Everard's mouth clamped into a tight hard line. "I never thought you desired lessons in how to act like a fool."

"But my accomplishments are quite lacking, sir." Aurelia simpered, continuing to goad him. "Why, you never even taught me the proper way to kiss."

The instant the words were spoken, Aurelia flushed, regretting it. Everard's eyes narrowed to points of steel.

"Then by all means," he said, his voice low, dangerous. "Allow me to complete your education."

Before she could move or cry out in protest, his arms were around her. . . . His mouth hovered above her lips for the barest instant, before crashing down to claim her lips. Aurelia was too stunned to put up more than a token struggle before she became lost in the bruising, sensual tempest of Everard's kiss. . . .

Fawcett Crest Books
by Susan Carroll:

THE LADY WHO HATED SHAKESPEARE

THE SUGAR ROSE

THE SUGAR ROSE

Susan Carroll

FAWCETT CREST • NEW YORK

A Fawcett Crest Book
Published by Ballantine Books
Copyright © 1987 by Susan Coppula

Library of Congress Catalog Card Number: 87-90842

ISBN 0-449-21238-6

Manufactured in the United States of America

First Edition: September 1987

To Kim Ostrom Bush,
a talented writer and good friend, in grateful ac-
knowledgment of all those late-night phone calls
that helped put the starch into Everard's cravats.

Chapter 1

"Aurelia Sinclair loves Lord Justin Spencer." The heat of a blush coursed into Aurelia's cheeks; her green eyes widened in mortification when she realized she had absentmindedly scrawled those words onto the flyleaf in her latest volume of Byron's poetry. Bad enough to indulge in such romantic nonsense when she was only fifteen, but at the sensible age of three and twenty, she ought to know better.

Justin, she reminded herself sternly, had not ridden to Sinclair Manor this morning to propose marriage as a result of any passionate devotion. No, he came only to do what had been long expected of him by both the Sinclair and Spencer families. If Aurelia looked for any warmer emotion from him other than friendship, then she was a fool.

"Giddings will be showing Lord Spencer upstairs at any moment now." The reedy voice of her elderly companion, Mrs. Elfreda Perkins, startled Aurelia from her unhappy thoughts. "Are you ready, my dear?"

Thrusting the book deep inside her workbasket, Aurelia straightened, raising one hand to the back of her head. Not so much as a strand of silken auburn hair escaped the crown of tightly woven braids. She tugged at the high-standing frills of her lace collar and shook out the folds of her saffron morning dress, wishing she had worn her comfortable, plain gray serge gown. The gossamer yards of clinging yellow furbelows did little to enhance her figure. But then, Aurelia thought with a grimace as she placed her hands upon her plump waistline, the fabric had yet to be woven that could accomplish that feat.

"I suppose I am as ready as I ever shall be." Her heart did a nervous flutter.

"Good. Then I shall whisk myself out of here." Effie said, tittering. She raised her brows in a look that was meant to be arch, but gave her more the appearance of a surprised owl. "I should be infinitely *de trop* when Lord Spencer drops to one knee and asks a certain question."

Effie stood on tiptoe to give Aurelia a swift kiss before skipping out of the sunlit music room. Aurelia winced. She thought it bad enough that Justin's mama had dropped "just a hint" to Aurelia herself to expect his lordship's proposal directly after breakfast, but it seemed that everyone from Effie down to the lowliest cook-maid was also privy to the secret that his lordship was *finally* coming to the point.

The sound of footsteps on the marble landing outside the door alerted Aurelia to the nearness of Justin's approach. Quickly she sat down upon the high-backed red velvet sofa, dragging her embroidery frame from her workbasket in an attempt to appear as if nothing occupied her mind except for the altar cloth she stitched to donate to the church.

If you had an ounce of pride, Aurelia Sinclair, she thought, you would refuse him. A man that comes to you at his mother's bidding!

But all such notions fled when the door swung open and she saw Justin's tall frame silhouetted in the entry. He grinned at her; his brown hair bleached light by the sun made a pleasing contrast to his bronzed skin.

"Good morning, Aurelia."

Before she could reply, Giddings pressed forward into the room, an affronted expression crossing his stately features. He announced in his frostiest accents, "Lord Spencer, miss."

Her pulses racing, Aurelia half rose, extending her hand.

"And," Giddings continued in tones of strong disapproval, "Mr. Everard Ramsey."

Aurelia sank back, as dismayed as Giddings by the sight of the immaculately tailored, dark-haired gentleman who followed Justin into the room. How often had Justin regaled her with tales of Everard Ramsey, whose meticulousness in matters of dress was only matched by his recklessness at the gaming tables! But why was Justin's friend so perverse as to call upon her this morning of all mornings, when Justin meant to propose?

Justin, however, did not appear in the least discomposed by Ramsey's untimely arrival. As he turned to greet his friend with every evidence of pleasure upon his handsome countenance, Aurelia struggled to suppress her own sense of bitter disappointment.

"I tried to keep the fellow out," Giddings said in an overly loud whisper. "But when he came tooling into the yard, he saw Lord Spencer's horse and knew that you were receiving—"

"Thank you, Giddings," Aurelia said quickly, fearful that Ramsey would overhear. "Would you please see to refreshment for my guests?"

"Certainly, miss." The old man made a dignified exit, muttering how a nice glass of arsenic would do for *some* persons who had not the wit to realize their timing was most inopportune.

Aurelia directed a weak smile at the two men. "I—I fear Giddings grows more eccentric with age."

Completely disconcerted by this unexpected turn of events, she shook hands with Justin before turning to murmur a greeting to Mr. Ramsey. She had taken a marked dislike to the man, although she had met him only the night before at supper. The London dandy had inspected her

3

across the table through his quizzing glass, studying her until Aurelia had been provoked into saying sweetly, "Pray, Mr. Ramsey, are you feeling quite the thing? My own dear papa was always wont to stare in just such a glazed fashion when he was about to suffer an attack of the gout."

The man hadn't even had the grace to blush, but her remark had had the effect of making him turn his gaze elsewhere, although she had the uncomfortable feeling that he followed every word of her conversation with Justin, her dinner partner.

After such an encounter, she would have thought that calling upon her would be the last notion to occur to Mr. Ramsey. 'Twas evident by his presence that she was quite wrong.

Ramsey executed a brief bow, his hooded blue eyes containing a hint of mockery. His perfectly formed jawline, his high cheekbones, his dark, arched brows gave the man an expression of carefully schooled arrogance. "I see my visit has taken you quite by surprise, Miss Sinclair." He produced a folded fan from the pocket of his flowered silk waistcoat. "You left this at my aunt's last evening, and she insisted I see it returned to you."

"What! The orderly, efficient Miss Sinclair forgetting her belongings." Justin chuckled. "That is most unlike the Reely I know."

Aurelia smiled at his teasing, but she felt her cheeks turn pink. Would she ever be able to persuade Justin to stop calling her by that dreadful childhood nickname?

"Thank you, Mr. Ramsey," she said, her hand clamping around the ivory handle. "But you need not have put yourself to such trouble, returning the fan immediately. Especially when I am sure you must have so *many more important matters* to attend to this morning."

"Here in the wilds of Norfolk, Miss Sinclair?" One of Ramsey's dark eyebrows shot upward. "No, I assure you

4

I have no pressing business whatsover. In fact, my entire day is at your disposal.''

He strode further into the room, stripping off his yellow kid gloves, giving every impression of intending to make a very long stay. His blue eyes glinted with what Aurelia would have called pure mischief if it had been anyone else but the stiffnecked Mr. Ramsey.

Justin pressed a small parcel into her hands. ''A trifling gift,'' he said, ''but 'tis something I know you like above all things.''

When Aurelia undid the string and the tissue wrapping fell away, she discovered a box of chocolates. Sweetmeats were ever a weakness with her, but her stomach was so knotted with apprehension and frustration, she had difficulty regarding Justin's gift with any sort of enthusiasm. Did Justin truly believe that was what she valued most in the world, sweetmeats? 'Twas obvious the insufferable Mr. Ramsey thought so from the way his cynical eyes shifted from the box to her waistline. In sheer defiance, she popped one of the sweet confections into her mouth before proffering the treat to the gentlemen, both of whom declined.

Ramsey held up his hand, feigning a shudder. ''No, thank you, Miss Sinclair. So early in the day! Incidentally, I do hope you do not find our calling thus soon after breakfast *inconvenient*?''

Hardly that, Aurelia felt like snapping. She had only been waiting five years for Justin to declare himself, ever since her father's death had left her orphaned. It seemed that, thanks to Mr. Ramsey, she must perforce wait a little longer.

''Inconvenient? Not at all, Mr. Ramsey,'' she forced herself to reply. She focused her attention upon Justin, affording him her most gracious smile. '' 'Tis prodigiously good to see *you* at any time, Justin. Pray, be seated.''

''I told you, did I not, Ev,'' Justin said, ''that Reely

would not be like one of your London belles, still lanquishing in bed at this hour of the day."

"One of *my* London belles?" Everard said so softly, Aurelia nearly did not catch the remark.

Justin glared at him, before favoring Aurelia with another of his heart-stopping smiles. He seated himself astride the reading chair, leaning his arms with careless grace upon the back of the book rest.

Was it truly so absurd, Aurelia thought wistfully, to hope that Justin did not view the prospect of marrying her with complete repugnance, that once wed, his childhood friendship with her might develop into emotions a trifle warmer? If there were any chance at all . . .

But her contemplation of Justin was seriously disturbed by Mr. Ramsey, who had chosen not to seat himself. What must the man do but pace about, examining the appointments of the room through his quizzing glass. As he regarded the faded Tree-of-Life wallpaper, the worn carpet, Aurelia almost wished she had elected to receive the gentlemen in one of the coldly elegant drawing rooms decorated by her mother. But of all the parlors in the rambling manor house, this was the one she had always considered peculiarly her own, where she felt the most secure. The massive fireplace mantel was not a showpiece designed by Adams, Gibbons, or anyone of note, but was constructed of good, plain oak, as were much of the room's furnishings. Best of all, the room had no mirrors to reflect back to her the imperfections of her less than willowy form.

Aurelia tossed her head. As if she cared a fig for Mr. Ramsey's opinion. Let him turn up his nose at her taste in decorating if he wished.

"I believe Trueblood strained a fetlock on our canter over here," Justin was saying. "I consigned him to the care of your head groom but I could scarce credit it. You still have old Harley working down in the stables. Why, he must be upward of seventy years old by now."

"O-oh, at least." Aurelia was vexed to discover she could not concentrate on Justin's words, so uncomfortable was Mr. Ramsey making her. After he trailed his fingers along the keys of the ancient rosewood pianoforte, his inspection of the room brought him over to the fireplace, in such close proximity Aurelia had to gather in her skirts to keep them from being trodden upon by his immaculate black Hessians. His cream-colored kerseymere trousers brushed up against her billowing yellow silk. With such closeness, Aurelia could not help remarking how his navy coat with mother-of-pearl buttons molded perfectly to his frame. Although he was not as tall and muscular as Justin, 'twas obvious the man had no need to resort to padding to fill out his shoulders.

"Don't you remember that, Reely?" Justin's impatient voice cut into her thoughts.

"What—I—I didn't quite hear you," she said. Embarrassed that Justin should find her so inattentive, she nervously ate several more chocolates.

"I was speaking of the time old Harley nearly took a switch to me, the time I stole a ride on your father's best hunter."

"Oh, that. Truly, Justin, you were always involved in so many pranks, 'tis difficult for me to remember them all."

Justin looked remarkably handsome as he threw back his head in a hearty laugh, but Aurelia was unable to enjoy fully the effect. The devil take Mr. Ramsey! If he must ruin everything this way, the least he could do would be to sit down and direct his supercilious stares from some forgotten corner. She noted with dread he was now examining the horrible collection of China jade figures assembled on the mantel.

"This fellow looks rather like a rabid bulldog. What is it for, Miss Sinclair? To ward off evil spirits?"

"If it is," she sighed, "it obviously does not work."

The corner of Ramsey's well-formed lips quivered, a ghost of a smile tipping his mouth. Then his features hardened into their customary sardonic expression.

Justin yawned. "Oh, do sit down, Ev, and let us talk about something else besides bric-a-brac."

"I should be only too happy to oblige," Ramsey drawled, "but I do not recall that I was ever invited to have a seat."

"Why, Mr. Ramsey, I—" Aurelia began indignantly, then halted in confusion. She *had* all but shown him the door when he arrived. Even considering her disappointment, such behavior was inexcusable.

She began to frame an awkward apology, when Justin interrupted, "Don't be such a cod's head, Ev. You needn't stand on ceremony here. Don't you know your aunt is Aurelia's god-mama? Why, both the Foxcliff and Spencer families have been acquainted with Reely forever and ever."

She grimaced. "Yes, I am just like the Tower of London. An ancient, well-known landmark."

Everard Ramsey emitted an odd, strangled sound. He muffled a sudden fit of coughing behind his hand.

"Oh, you know what I meant, Aurelia." Justin gave her a look of smiling exasperation.

"I am afraid I do," she murmured. "Please forgive me, Mr. Ramsey, if I have been remiss in my duties as hostess. Of course, you are quite welcome to sit down."

Indeed she was beginning to feel a little ashamed of herself for her uncivil behavior. The emotion quickly vanished when Mr. Ramsey ignored all the bandy-legged Queen Anne chairs and settled himself beside her on the sofa. The quizzing glass that had been fixed upon the mantel ornaments was now trained as mercilessly upon her face.

She gulped down two more chocolates and hauled her stitchery up onto her lap in an effort to maintain a calm demeanor. How piercingly blue the man's eyes were, the deep vivid blue of the sky on a crisp autumn afternoon. And his hair. Strange that she had not remarked it before. Those glossy midnight waves absolutely refused to remain swept into the neat Brutus style so popular amongst the gentlemen. It must be a source of deep chagrin to the particular Mr. Ramsey.

"Your ability with the needle is remarkable, Miss Sinclair." The sound of his voice startled her. "However do you contrive to take such delicate stitches without looking at your work?"

Aurelia nearly stabbed herself as she realized she had been staring at him as intensely as he regarded her. She lowered her eyes, but she determined not to allow Ramsey to intimidate her further.

" 'Tis all a matter of practice," she said. "Just as I am sure that is how you acquired your skill with a quizzing glass. Could I persuade you to level it at the carpet? I seem to have dropped one of my needles."

"Alas, Miss Sinclair, you overrate my ability. I have never been good at retrieving lost articles." But he did lower his glass, dangling it by the ribbon between two of his graceful, tapering fingers.

From across the room Justin muffled a yawn. Aurelia feared he was bored by the conversation, but she saw that he scarce attended to herself and Mr. Ramsey. Justin's gaze traveled to the tall windows, and Aurelia knew instinctively he regarded the fields, the woodland beyond. 'Twas perfect hunting weather. He shifted restlessly in his seat. It would not be long before he would be making his excuses, drawing his visit to a close.

Plague take Everard Ramsey! Aurelia forcefully jabbed her needle into the linen cloth and reached for another chocolate. She almost wished Giddings *would* slip a little arsenic into the man's Madeira.

Ramsey leaned forward for a closer inspection of her

work. "What is that you are sewing with such great energy?"

She was seized by a strange urge to shake him out his air of imperturbability. " 'Tis a shroud," she said primly.

Her words had the desired effect. Ramsey jerked upright, his eyes widening. "I—I beg your pardon? Er, sewing shrouds—surely that is a rather unusual occupation for a young lady?"

"I like to be prepared. One never knows when there will be a sudden demise in one's circle of acquaintance."

The elusive smile played across his features. "If you are thinking of me, then you had best be like Penelope and take your time about it. I am made of sturdier stuff than you might imagine."

"I may follow her example and unravel a little each night," Aurelia conceded. "But I refuse to stretch it out twenty years for you."

Despite herself, she was beginning to enjoy the verbal sparring, when Justin rose abruptly to his feet, stretching his long limbs. "I warn the two of you, if you commence talking about a bunch of musty Romans, I will be off at once."

"Greeks, my dear fellow," Ramsey said. "The story of Penelope and Odysseus is from Greece."

Justin shrugged. " 'Tis all one to me. I think it much better if we get to the purpose of my visit." He fished inside his waistcoat pocket. A look of annoyance crossed his tanned features. "Hang it all. I have forgotten the ring."

Aurelia froze, her needle poked halfway into a stitch, a rising sensation of horror taking possession of her. No! Surely not! Justin could not be meaning to carry on with his proposal, not under the critical eyes of Everard Ramsey.

After patting his coat pockets, Justin threw up his hands. "Oh, well, I can always bring the ring by another day. The important thing is to settle when the banns will be cried and set a date." He paused, flashing his most engagingly boyish grin. "By the bye, Reely, you do wish to marry me, don't you?"

"I—I . . ." She opened her mouth, but the words refused to come. She felt the color flood into her face, hurt, embarrassment, and anger warring within her breast.

Everard Ramsey heaved himself to his feet. "This is the outside of enough! Even for you, Justin." His face flushed, Ramsey took an awkward step backward, kicking over Aurelia's workbasket. The contents spilled to the floor, unnoticed by him as he spluttered, "To—to be making Miss Sinclair an offer with me sitting here!" An expression of extreme irritation crossed his fine-chiseled features. "Ah, I see. 'Tis another one of your pranks, Justin. You and Miss Sinclair are making a May game of me."

"Not at all. Aurelia and I are completely serious," Justin said. "Are we not, Aurelia?"

"Y-yes." At least, *she* was. She could not decide who infuriated her more, Justin, with his thoughtlessness, or Mr. Ramsey, who believed the mere idea of Justin marrying her would have to be in the nature of a jest. She started to rise, longing to give both of them a good setdown, but even after all these years, the icy voice of her mother echoed inside her head. *A lady, Aurelia, never loses her temper.*

She took a deep breath to steady herself, counting backward in French.

Ramsey glowered at Justin. "I think you might defer this to a more appropriate moment."

"Completely, unnecessary, sir," Aurelia broke in. Aye, doubtless the fashionable Mr. Ramsey hoped that, in the meantime, he might be able to prevent his friend's becoming engaged to such a dowdy, unattractive female. She raised her chin to stare defiantly into Ramsey's blue eyes. "Of course, I will accept your offer, Justin. With the greatest of pleasure."

Ramsey's lips compressed into a rigid line of disapproval, which only seemed to deepen when Justin strode over and clapped him on the back.

"Excellent. Then everything is settled. Why put yourself into such a taking, Ev? Reely is not in the least offended by the manner of my proposal, so why should you be?"

"If Miss Sinclair is not offended, then she ought to be. Even in an arranged marriage, there are certain courtesies, certain expressions of sentiment—"

"Don't be ridiculous. Reely and I are old friends. Our estates march alongside each other. Our marriage has been expected for years. Why, Reely is not in the least romantic. She would laugh in my face if I were to drop to one knee and spout a parcel of sentimental nonsense to her, would you not, old fellow?"

Aurelia swallowed before answering with a lightness she was far from feeling. "I don't know. It might prove quite useful if you were to kneel on the carpet. You might chance to alight upon the needle I dropped."

Justin chuckled, turning to flash a triumphant grin at his friend. Ramsey's face settled into a mask of indifference. " 'Twould seem the pair of you are well suited. Permit me to offer my felicitations."

"Too kind of you, I'm sure," Aurelia said with a brittle smile. Her satisfaction in having nettled Mr. Ramsey faded along with all her daydreams that Justin would somehow learn to return her feelings of love. When would she ever learn that romance was not for such a one as she? But maybe if Ramsey had not been present, Justin would have been more . . . No, she feared he would have proceeded in the same graceless manner. Justin would always be Justin, and there was naught that would ever change him. Were not his unpredictability, his lack of regard for the conventions, all part of his charm?

A friendship, a marriage of convenience, was all he desired. She would have to learn to accept that if she meant to be his wife. Fortunately she had never worn her heart on her sleeve. Justin need never know of her love for him. Mayhap she had not enough pride to refuse his offer, but she had enough to conceal that folly from him. She ate a few more chocolates and returned to her stitching, trying to appear as casual about the morning's events as Justin did.

The two men busied themselves righting her workbasket, gathering up the pincushion, thread, and skeins of yarn. Ramsey straightened, examining a small leather-bound volume

"You astonish me, Miss Sinclair. I would not have thought anyone as unromantic as you proclaim yourself to be would have a taste for Byronic poetry."

With a sinking sensation she realized Ramsey had gotten hold of her edition of *The Corsair*. It must have fallen out when the workbasket tipped.

"Oh, no! I—I mean that belongs to my companion." She snatched it out of his hands just as he was opening the book to the flyleaf.

Ramsey looked considerably surprised when she stuffed the volume behind the sofa cushion, leaning against it. Better that he should think her a bit touched in the upper works than he should read that foolish inscription. How his lip would curl in scorn.

"I shall have to tell Effie to be more careful with her books," she said.

"Indeed." Ramsey hooded his eyes, the look in them unfathomable.

Justin rubbed his hands together. "I suppose I should hasten back to Penborough to convey the glad tidings to my mother and Clarice."

"Yes," Aurelia said dryly. "Only fancy how astounded they will be."

Justin laughed. "Ah, Reely, that is what I like best about you. You are such a jokesmith."

"Truly. I am so amusing, I laugh at myself, sometimes." The words nearly caught in her throat. If only he and Mr. Ramsey would leave. Her smile was feeling strained, and absurd tears were beginning to prickle at the back of her eyes. She prepared to see the gentlemen out, but as she tried to set her needlework aside, she was appalled to realize she had sewn all the way through the linen into the fabric of her dress.

Aurelia nearly groaned aloud. 'Twas as if the Fates conspired this morning to make her appear a total fool. She settled the frame back onto her lap, hoping that neither Justin nor Mr. Ramsey—especially not Mr. Ramsey—had noticed.

"Forgive me if I don't see you to the door," she croaked, "since we do not stand on ceremony here."

Justin smiled, his mind apparently on nothing more than escape. He bent over and placed a chaste kiss upon her cheek, assuring her he would call upon her again very soon. The kiss was so far from what she had hoped for after his proposal that her heart did not even skip a beat.

She felt a surge of relief as he strode toward the door, but Everard Ramsey seemed determined to discomfit her to the last. While she sat with her hands draped awkwardly over the linen, trying to pretend nothing was amiss, the man lingered. Finding another spool of thread, he leisurely replaced it in her sewing basket before ducking into a low bow to make his farewells.

"Thank you for a most, er, interesting morning, Miss Sinclair. I hope we will meet again, soon."

And I hope you choke on your own cravat, she thought. Aloud, she said, "So nice of you to call. Good day, sir."

"Come along, Ev," Justin called from the threshold. "If I cannot ride Trueblood, I may need you to take me up in your curricle."

14

As though oblivious of Justin's impatience, Ramsey slowly raised one of Aurelia's hands and carried it briefly to his lips. Struggling to appear composed, she dared not move until the music room door closed behind the two men.

"Thank God," she said. No matter how disastrous the rest of the morning had been, at least she could congratulate herself upon having hoodwinked the sharp-eyed Mr. Ramsey. She relaxed, allowing her hands to fall back into her lap. 'Twas then she realized Ramsey had somehow found opportunity for dropping an object on top of the stitchery.

Her lips curved into a rueful smile as her fingers closed over her scissors.

Chapter 2

The curricle's iron-rimmed wheels rumbled perilously near the edge of the ditch. Justin lurched against the side of the open-top carriage, then made a frantic grab for the back of his seat.

"Damnation, Everard! Watch what you are about."

Everard directed an angry sidelong glare at his friend. Gritting his teeth, he slapped the reins against the backs of the sprightly pair of chestnuts between the traces. Fields broken into neat squares by hedgerows and mounds of hay being harvested into tall ricks all flashed by in a blur of green and gold.

Justin stared down at the ditch, bracing himself for the accident to come, but somehow Everard managed to guide the vehicle back onto the road just as the rear wheel careened a hairsbreadth over the edge.

When the curricle resumed its pace down the center of the country lane, Justin straightened. "Blast you, Ev! I'll never know how any man who is so cool and circumspect in the saddle can be such a madman when it comes to handling the ribbons."

"If you don't like the way I drive, you can always walk," Everard snapped, still seething over the embarrassing trick Justin had served him that morning. Forcing him to witness that travesty of a marriage proposal! He urged the horse on faster, sending the curricle rattling through a series of bone-jarring ruts. Mud spattered up over the wheels, just missing the toes of Everard's gleaming Hessians, but managing to bespeckle the hems of Justin's buff-colored trousers.

"By God," Justin groaned. "I believe I would have done better to borrow one of Reely's horses or to have led Trueblood back across the fields." His eyes rolled nervously toward the ditch. "Damn it, Ev. Keep toward the center. That side of the road is completely washed out."

Everard turned a deaf ear to the warning. The devil take Justin, he thought. There was nothing Everard hated worse than being involved in any sort of a scene. For once in his life, Justin might have employed a modicum of decency, of common sense, of—

"Dash it, Ev. Hard to the left. To the left. Ow!" Lord Spencer swore. Lunging forward, he reached across Everard and seized the reins, yanking until the horse halted in the center of the road.

The muscles in Everard's face went rigid with suppressed anger. In carefully controlled tones, he said, "If any other man besides you had dared do that—"

"I know." Justin panted. "You would run him through. Have mercy, Ev. I don't mind attempting to break my own neck, but I very much object to someone else doing it for me."

His teeth flashed into a broad grin, which Everard returned with a stone-faced regard. "You needn't have feared," he said icily. "I would never permit anything to happen to Aunt Lydia's best curricle." He gazed pointedly to where Justin's fingers still gripped the reins. Justin released the leather straps and slumped back in his seat. Everard set the carriage into motion again. Although his irritation with Justin continued to gnaw at him, he managed to keep the chestnuts to a sedate trot.

"So what the devil have I done now to put you in such

a bad skin?'' Justin asked. "Surely you're not still fuming about that night I paid Moll Periwinkle a guinea to sneak into your bed?"

Everard grimaced at the remembrance of waking to feel bony elbows and knees digging into his back, a mouth reeking of cabbage and garlic nibbling at his ear.

"No, until you mentioned it, I had contrived to forget that particular incident. To be sure, I did not find it half so diverting as the time you put the pepper in my snuffbox."

Justin stretched out his long limbs as much as the curricle would permit, a lazy smile touching his lips at the memory, a smile completely lacking in repentence. Everard heaved a sigh of exasperation. At the age of twenty-eight, he was but two years Justin's senior. Why, sometimes, did he feel as if it were fifty?

"Then I can't understand—" Justin broke off. "Good Lord, you cannot still be grousing over what happened with Reely this morning."

"Not at all. Your affair entirely, old friend. I have only this to say. The next time you propose marriage to some wench, be so good as to leave me out of it."

"I trust there won't be a next time." Justin gave him a playful jab on the arm. "What's come over you, Ev? I have never known you to get in such a pelter over anything so trivial."

"Trivial?" Everard nearly choked on the word. It took great restraint on his part to keep his hands steady. "Oh, aye, the whole affair was so trivial you never thought to warn me what you were going to do. If I had had the least notion, I would have excused myself at once. You place me in a dashed awkward position."

"You live in your own world, Ramsey." Justin chuckled. "You must have been the only person in the shire who did not know the nature of my business with Reely this morning."

18

"Damn it! Don't keep calling her that! She has a perfectly lovely first name."

Justin gaped at him, but he looked no more astonished than Everard was feeling himself at his outburst.

"Sorry," Everard muttered. "As I said before, entirely your own affair." He shook his head, trying to sift his way through a confusing mélange of emotions. Justin was well within his rights to ask. What *had* come over him? He had been in perfectly good humor when he had first arrived at Sinclair Manor, looking forward to furthering his acquaintance with Miss Sinclair. The woman was an original if Everard had ever met one. Yet his chagrin over what had actually taken place was scant excuse for his present state of agitation.

"I'll tell you what 'tis, old fellow," Justin spoke up suddenly. "You have been rusticating in Norfolk so long, you're getting frayed at the edges. Too many evenings of playing whist for a penny a point with these fat country squires. What you need is to return to town, get back to the tables at Watier's."

"I suppose so, although London would be mighty thin of company at this time of year." Everard forced a smile to his lips, but it continued to disturb him that he had reacted so strongly to the little scene played out before him that morning. Why could he not forget about it?

'Twas most likely because of that damned book. He had had only the barest glimpse of the inscription on the flyleaf: "Aurelia Sinclair loves—" But it hadn't been difficult to guess the rest. In unguarded moments, Aurelia Sinclair's heart surfaced in those remarkable green eyes of hers, revealing a sensitive woman hiding her wounds beneath a veil of wit and jest.

"Damme!" Everard muttered under his breath, cursing the talent he had for discovering secrets. Why was he afflicted with this uncanny perception that saw beyond the facades others presented, probing too deep into their private guilt and pain? 'Twould be so much more comfortable to saunter through life as Justin did, blissfully deaf and blind to his neighbors' heartaches.

Though at the moment, Everard noted wryly, Justin was looking far from being shortsighted. Lord Spencer's eyes nearly bulged from their sockets as he ogled a buxom dairymaid. As they passed the field where the girl led her cows to pasture, she ducked in a respectful curtsy. She put an additional sway into her full hips and blushingly bobbed in Justin's direction. Justin grinned and swept her a salute with his high-crowned beaver hat.

How did they always know, these women, that Justin was so susceptible to a pretty face? Ever since Everard had first become acquainted with Lord Spencer during their days at Oxford, he had pondered the question with no satisfactory answer. 'Twas as if there was some undefinable mutual allure between Justin and any attractive creature in skirts.

Everard slapped down on the reins, urging the horses to pick up speed again, leaving the amply endowed dairymaid behind them. Justin craned his neck for a last look.

"So you are planning to get leg-shackled at last," Everard said sharply to gain Justin's attention. "At least that will put an end to Lady Sylvie Fitzhurst's determined efforts to fix your interest." The thought filled Everard with a sense of great relief. Sylvie Fitzhurst, in his estimation, was a sly, grasping creature, more noted for her dazzling blond looks than her discretion. Any liaison with that baggage would only have led Justin into more trouble.

But Justin's brows jutted upward in surprise at Everard's statement. "What has my forthcoming marriage to do with Sylvie? I am hoping that in the next month or so our flirtation will develop into something far warmer."

"I see you have laid your plans well. A new bride and a new mistress. How damnable convenient and timesaving,

20

too! You can select a wedding gift for Aurelia at the same time as you pick up a few trinkets for Lady Sylvie."

"What a capital notion." Lights of mischief danced in Justin's eyes. "And stop screwing up your face in that manner. You look as priggish as a parson about to deliver a lecture."

"I would if I thought 'twould be of any avail. Have you given one moment's thought as to how Miss Sinclair will feel about this proposed arrangement of yours?"

Justin shrugged. "She would not much care, as long as I am discreet. I've explained to you repeatedly, this is a marriage of convenience, not the grande passion. All Reely expects from me is my title and a nursery full of children."

"Aye. Doubtless, you are correct." Everard grimaced. Most likely that was all Aurelia expected from Justin. But what she might long for, dream of, was entirely a different matter. An image of her flashed through Everard's mind, the curve of her lips quivering into a wistful smile, a wistfulness she quickly concealed behind a too ready laugh.

"You will, I trust, at least remember to take her the ring, will you not?" he asked.

Justin yawned and stretched again. "Oh, aye. I'll remember. Because I know you will give me little peace until I do. The trouble with you, Ev, is that beneath your pose of cynical dandy lurks the heart of a true romantic." His chest rumbled with another deep chuckle. "Lord, after the way you twitted Reely about having a copy of *The Corsair*, how she would laugh if I told her about your own dog-eared copies of Byron, to say nothing of Sir Walter Scott."

Everard felt a tinge of red rise into his cheeks, but he contrived to say lightly, "I beg you will not. I am in enough difficulties without having my reputation destroyed as well."

The laughter swiftly died out of Justin's eyes; his smiling lips set into an expression of unaccustomed somberness. He shifted his gaze away from Everard, appearing to be deeply engrossed by a drainage windmill they were passing, the arms twirling slowly like a lazy giant guarding the land. Lord Spencer cleared his throat. "About your difficulties, Ev, you know I would be happy to lend you—"

"No!" In milder tones, Everard continued, "No, I thank you, all the same. I have not yet sunk to the point of borrowing from my friends."

"But you could pay me back—with interest—as soon as your ship comes in."

"My ship." Everard gave a mirthless bark of laughter. "The only way you would recover your loan from my assets on *The Albatross* is if you are capable of holding your breath for a very long time and diving to the bottom of the sea."

"You don't know that for certain. Why, it has only been—"

"One year, ten months, and seventeen days," Everard said flatly. The exact amount of time since he had stood on the dock in Portsmouth and watched *The Albatross*'s billowing white sails skim over the horizon, carrying with her all his hopes, his dreams, and nigh every penny of the modest fortune he had inherited through his grandfather's trust.

"The Folly" his father, Sir Fitzwilliam Ramsey, had dubbed *The Albatross*. "Outfitting merchant vessels for trade with Brazil," he had snorted. "You may as well fling your fortune away on a turn of the cards and be done with it. Didn't you hear what happened to those speculators who put their money in the cargo of *The Royal George*? Scarce enough money left now to buy breeches to cover their privies."

"The Royal George, Father?" Everard had countered in tones of long-suffering patience. "Do you know what cargo they carried? Wool blankets, warming pans, and ice skates! Ice skates to Brazil, for the love of God! We propose to outfit *The Albatross* with lightweight cottons. Brazil has no cotton manufactories."

"I don't give a hang what a parcel of brown-faced heathens have or don't have." Sir Fitz's large peppery mustache fairly bristled with his wrath. Then he uttered his clincher to every argument. "If your brother Arthur had lived, he would never have done anything so foolish."

If Arthur had lived. Everard thought he had heard those words a damn sight too often.

"Ev. Watch out!"

Justin's outcry of warning pierced through Everard's unhappy reverie. He snapped back to the present in time to realize the curricle had rounded the bend and was bearing down upon a pony cart. Everard pulled on the reins, attempting to guide his carriage off to the side. But 'twas already too late. The wheels of the two vehicles slammed together, and Everard's own curses resounded in his ears along with the crack of splintering wood.

The late afternoon sun glinted through the tall windows, sparkling on the silver tea service, but the rich brew tasted remarkably bitter to Aurelia, despite the quantity of sugar she spooned into the delicate Wedgwood cup.

Glumly she regarded the small parcel that had just arrived, delivered by Justin's groom. As she opened the brief note that accompanied it, Justin's bold hand fairly leaped off the page, all but illegible.

Reely,

Everard is still haranguing me about my lack of regard for the formalities, so I thought I'd better dispatch Crowley to bring you the ring posthaste.

Aye, Aurelia thought with a touch of asperity, since the groom was coming to fetch Trueblood, in any case. Then, scolding herself for her cynicism she read on.

Would have brought it myself, but Ev and I suffered a coaching accident on the way home. Not to

*worry. I have taken no serious injury. As to the ring,
Mama thought you might like to have one of the family
jewels, so I selected one that you have always
particularly admired. Her ladyship has been troubled
of late with a touch of the megrim, but shall be calling upon you within the next day or two to set the
date for making me the happiest of men.*

> *Yours,*
>
> *J.*

Aurelia bit her lip as she anxiously perused the note one
more time. Wasn't that exactly like Justin to toss out such
an alarming piece of news as a carriage accident and then
not explain himself more fully? She was forced to suppose
from the tone of his letter that all was as he said, that he
truly had not sustained any injury. But what of Mr. Ramsey? Justin said nothing of how he had fared.

Her fingers tightened on the brief missive. As if she
cared what became of Mr. Ramsey, in any case. Detestable
man! Doubtless he was quite unscathed and still laughing
to himself over her clumsy error in sewing her gown to the
altar cloth. Yet, doubts arose to dispel the unpleasant image. If Ramsey were determined to be amused at her ex-
pense, why had he slipped her the scissors, thus sparing
her further embarrassment? 'Twas in truth an act of great
consideration, not in the least what she would have expected from him. Mayhap her initial impression of the man
as an arrogant coxcomb was entirely too harsh.

Still puzzling over Ramsey's actions, she refolded the
note and set it down upon her tea tray before turning her
attention to the small box. As she undid the wrapping, she
stared in disbelief at the gaudy ruby that blinked amid a
circle of diamonds and emeralds.

"Good Lord." She groaned. One of the family jewels!
'Twas more like one of the family antiquities. When had

Justin ever gotten the notion that she had admired such a thing?

To be sure, she did recall a remark she'd once made upon first seeing the ring amongst the collection of treasures at Penborough Castle. "Upon my word, what a stunning ring. I feel quite stunned just looking at it."

Never had one of her jests been so appallingly misconstrued, Aurelia thought ruefully as she lifted the heavy band from its velvet-lined case. She crinkled her nose in distaste. The ring's hideous vulgarity was not its worst aspect. The most dreadful consideration was that the jewel truly was priceless, an heirloom dating from the time of Henry VIII. How would she ever face Justin's mama if she were to lose it?

So absorbed was she by this gloomy prospect that she scarce noticed when Giddings entered the room, until he coughed discreetly. She looked up to find the elderly retainer's face positively thunderous with disapproval.

"Begging your pardon, miss, but there is a person below stairs absolutely insistent upon seeing you."

"A person?" she repeated. Now who would Giddings describe in such terms? The answer came to her in a rush, sending a blush coursing into her cheeks. Who else but Everard Ramsey? 'Twas past all belief that the man should have the effrontery to call upon her twice in the same day, uninvited. Had he returned to tease her about the dress incident or mayhap to see if there was yet some way to prevent her engagement to Justin?

No, it could hardly be that, or he would not have urged Justin to send her the ring. Nervously, she patted her hair and rammed the large ruby upon her finger. Well, whatever his motives for coming, she would not permit Mr. Ramsey to discompose her so easily this time.

Scarce thinking what she did, she wolfed down one of the tea cakes and said, "Show Mr. Ramsey upstairs at once, Giddings."

Her butler looked as if he thought she had taken leave of her senses. "Why, I did not say a word about Mr. Ramsey, miss."

"Oh." An unexpected sense of disappointment surged through her. "Then who—"

" 'Tis that person who has recently leased Wetherbee Hall." Giddings sniffed. "I put him in the Blue Salon," he added in much the same tones he would have used to describe dropping a dead rat into the refuse heap.

"Mr. Augustus Snape?" Aurelia winced. A gazetted fortune hunter of the worst stamp, Mr. Snape had recently taken up residence in Norfolk, reputedly because he had met with no luck snaring a wealthy bride in London.

"I don't suppose you could simply tell him I died," she said, "or at least have contracted an extremely contagious case of the scarlet fever."

Giddings folded his hands, raising his eyes to the sculpted ceiling. "Certainly, if it is your wish, miss, I could tell him you had been taken ill. However, in your late mother's time . . ."

He left the sentence unfinished, but Aurelia had no difficulty in completing the thought. In her late mother's time, no visitors were ever turned away from Sinclair Manor, not even a man as disagreeable as the oily-tongued Mr. Snape.

"A lady, Aurelia," her mother had alway said, "never stoops to subterfuge to rid herself of unwelcome guests. Rather, she receives the visitors and treats them to such a display of chilling dignity, they never dare call again."

Aurelia heaved a deep sigh. "I shall be down directly, Giddings."

"Very good, miss." Giddings made a wooden bow and stalked out of the room.

Aurelia rose and slowly wended her way down the curving red-carpeted stair to the lower floor. She attempted to school her features into an expression of hauteur but gave over the attempt when she caught a glimpse of herself in the hall mirror.

" 'Tis impossible for a woman with a dimpled chin to look chilling," she grumbled. She was tempted to send for Effie. At least the presence of her elderly companion would restrain Mr. Snape from becoming too carried away with his compliments and fawning over her hand. But Effie was still lying down, so overcome had the volatile little woman been by the tidings of Lord Spencer's proposal.

Loath to disturb her companion and berating herself as a coward, Aurelia resolutely shoved open the door and stepped into the Blue Salon. The gangly form of Mr. Snape looked strangely out of place, his plum-colored jacket and apple-green waistcoat clashing with the muted elegance of the blue velvet swag draperies. From above the ornate marble fireplace, the portraits of her parents, her florid, portly father, her reed-thin, hawk-eyed mother, both seemed to regard Snape's presence at Sinclair Manor with extreme disapproval.

Snape stood with one hand held stiffly against his back, while his other cadaverlike hand examined a Sevres vase balanced on a delicate Queen Anne table, his fingernails pinging against the china.

"I assure you 'tis quite genuine, Mr. Snape," Aurelia said dryly.

Snape whirled his head around as fast as his high starched collar and stiff cravat would permit. His pale complexion put Aurelia in mind of the Broadland eels who slithered out of their wintery beds each April.

"Ah, Miss Sinclair. I—I was just admiring this magnificent piece. Your taste is so very similiar to that of my third cousin, the Marquess of Scallingsforth."

Aurelia fixed a rigid smile upon her lips and extended her hand with what she hoped was a duchesslike dignity. Snape strode over and pressed cold, thin lips against her knuckles. Aurelia grimaced as she felt the prickles of tiny, stiff chin whiskers scrape against her flesh. Mr. Snape had made a poor job of shaving that morning. 'Twas rumored his valet had run off with the chambermaid a fortnight ago, taking many of the Snape family valuables with them. At least that was the excuse Mr. Snape had given for why there was no silverplate present at the last dinner party given at Wetherbee Hall.

As Mr. Snape was raising his mouth from her hand, he froze, the facets of the ruby ring sparking red gleams in his narrow eyes.

"Why, Miss Sinclair. What a stunning ring."

"Indeed," she murmured. "Exactly the description I would have chosen myself." Fearing that at any moment, he might begin to drool over her fingers, Aurelia swiftly withdrew her hand.

"Pray be seated, sir, and tell me to what I owe the honor of this visit." She silently congratulated herself upon the frosty accents with which she delivered this speech, but when Mr. Snape pursed his lips together until he resembled an emaciated mackerel, she nigh ruined the entire effect by erupting into laughter.

"I do not know if you will deem this visit an honor or not, when I tell you the reason for it," Snape said in solemn tones, placing one hand over his heart. "But, pray, believe me it is only my concern for your reputation that has driven me hither."

"My reputation?" Aurelia echoed as she settled herself upon the stiff silk cushions of a French sofa. Whatever was the man talking about?

Snape raked bony fingers back through his slick thatch-colored hair, then took a few quick turns before the hearth before stopping to proclaim dramatically, "My dear Miss Sinclair, I fear rumors of a most scandalous nature have reached my ears. It pains me to distress you, but I have been hearing talk in the village of how you, a lady of quality, have been entertaining gentlemen of the most reprehensible character. Rakes, libertines, gamesters!''

Aurelia's mouth twitched. "Dear me. I do not recall receiving any such gentlemen. They must have called when I was not at home. How very disappointing.''

Snape fixed her with a reproachful stare. "You pretend that you have not been visited by Lord Spencer and Mr. Everard Ramsey, when I know for a fact they were here only this morning.''

Aurelia stifled an indignant gasp. Of all the insufferable impertinence. Had this odious creature been spying upon the Manor? Let this be a lesson to take care in future whom she spoke to at assemblies, even when someone as unexceptionable as the vicar performed the introduction. She rose to her feet.

"Mr. Snape. I fail to see how it concerns you whom I receive or do not. Now, I fear I am obliged to bid you good—''

She broke off as Snape abruptly changed his tactics. His colorless eyes damp with remorse, he vaulted across the room to her side and began groping for her hands. For one dreadful moment, Aurelia feared he meant to drop to one knee before her.

"Please. Do not be wroth with me, dear lady. If I seemed too abrupt, too forward in my remarks, 'tis only because I find myself so overwhelmed by your numerous charms.'' Snape sighed gustily, stealing longing glances at the ruby glittering on her finger.

"P-pray, sir, strive for some command of yourself,'' Aurelia said in a voice that was not quite steady.

But he continued to struggle for possession of her hand. "I know you are far too innocent to realize what the presence of such a notorious womanizer as Lord Spencer—''

Aurelia yanked her hand away. "I must warn you that when you speak of Lord Spencer, you are speaking of the man I am going to marry.''

29

"What!" Snape rocked back on his heels, his countenance waxing even more ghostlike.

Dear God, Aurelia thought. The man looked as if he were about to swoon, and she had not the least notion where any smelling salts were to be found.

"I am going to marry Lord Spencer," she repeated more gently.

Snape staggered a few steps backward, striking one hand to his forehead. "No, I cannot believe it. Fate could not deal me such a blow."

Aurelia quirked an eyebrow, wondering if, somewhere in Mr. Snape's highly dubious background, the man had trod the boards at Drury Lane.

"I can assure you it is true," she said. "The understanding between Lord Spencer and myself has been one of long duration. You yourself have already remarked upon my betrothal ring."

"But—but I had already informed my creditors—I mean my family—that you and I, that we . . . ." Snape stared at her, then slowly lowered his hand. 'Twas as if he lowered a mask at the same time. An ugly red began to seep up his neck, suffusing his thin face, until Aurelia was about to suggest it might be expedient if he were to loosen his cravat.

"So," he growled, "then all this time you have been toying with me, trifling with my affections!"

"I would scarce call dancing with you at the assembly and permitting you to fetch me punch as trifling with—"

"You led me on, you jade." Snape leveled a shaking finger at her. "You permitted me to entertain false hopes."

"I did nothing of the kind! And now, sir, I must really insist that you leave." She strode across the room and yanked on the bell pull one time before Snape bounded after her. He seized her by the wrist and spun her around.

Dropping all efforts to speak with his usual cultivated purr, he shouted, "Oh, no, 'twill take more than that scrawny old butler to toss me out before I've had my say. No one makes a fool of Gus Snape. Especially not after I spent a fortune sending you roses.''

Aurelia cried out in shock as much as pain when he twisted her wrist in his bony grasp. She had regarded Snape as nothing more than an ingratiating buffoon. Never would she have guessed him capable of such violence. The man was quite mad, and as he thrust his protuberant nose close to her face, for the first time she detected the odor of sour gin upon his breath.

"I thought a fat old spinster like you would have jumped at the chance to marry me." He sneered. "Never guessed you already had a lord on the string.''

Aurelia flushed, raising her free hand almost reflexively, preparing to deal a strong clout to Snape's ear. But beyond her, the frozen stare of her mother's portrait already seemed to be rebuking her for allowing this scene to get so far beyond the bounds of dignity.

Aurelia lowered her arm, striving for icy scorn between clenched teeth. "Sir, I demand you release me at once.''

"No country-bred wench gets the better of me. We shall see how high and mighty you are, Miss Sinclair, when I am done with you. I'll have my vengeance. You can bank upon it. I—''

He broke off as the parlor door opened. "Get out of here, you old fool," he snarled, wrenching his head in the direction.

"Giddings," Aurelia cried out, tugging futilely to free herself.

But 'twas not the old man who had answered the bell. The young footman, James, his burly arms already outgrowing his smart new livery, stood silhouetted in the entry. He eyed Mr. Snape, his mouth splitting into a grin of unholy anticipation at the prospect of a mill. "Miss Aurelia? Was there something you was wanting?''

31

Snape flinched, dropping her arm as if it were a firebrand.

"Yes, James," Aurelia said, rubbing her bruised flesh. "I believe Mr. Snape requires some assistance in finding the front door."

"Right, miss." James doubled two large meaty fists. Snape stumbled backward, his eyes bulging as the grinning young man advanced upon him.

"Uh, no, not at all. Quite a misunderstanding. M-most sorry, Miss Sinclair, to have troubled you. I—I'll just be going now."

Snape circled around James and bolted from the room, the man's previous attitude of menace vanishing as rapidly as his flapping coattails.

"Why, what a wretched, cowardly bully!" Aurelia exclaimed.

"I'll just follow him, miss," James said hopefully, "and make sure he doesn't get lost."

"That is not necessary. I trust we have seen the last of Mr. Snape." Aurelia took a deep breath. "What you could do is fetch me a very large glass of sherry."

"Of course, miss." Looking considerably crestfallen, James lumbered out of the parlor, leaving Aurelia to collapse back down upon the French sofa. The encounter had left her more shaken than she would have imagined. She had never in her life been insulted in so vulgar a fashion, let alone suffered any physical abuse from one passing himself off as a gentleman. How had such a weasel as Augustus Snape ever managed to gain entré into polite circles?

Her gaze traveled to the portrait of the slender, sharp-faced beauty above mantle. "Well, Mama, and to think you always told me that I was not the sort that would ever break hearts."

Aurelia emitted a weak chuckle as she raised her hand, staring at the heavily jeweled ring. "In future, I shall have to take care that my abundant charms are not so lavishly displayed.'' A shudder coursed through her as she remembered Snape's spiteful expressions, the nasty glint in his eye as he had threatened vengeance. What would she do if he persisted in troubling her further?

For a moment, she almost thought of sending for Justin, informing him of Snape's insulting behavior. But she feared Lord Spencer would be driven to deal with Mr. Snape in an exceedingly rash and violent manner, stirring up no end of scandal. Now, a gentleman like Everard Ramsey . . . She closed her eyes. She could easily picture Mr. Ramsey dispatching Snape with cool efficiency, the villain cringing before Ramsey's hard stare, withering under his steel-edged scorn.

Startled by her imaginings, Aurelia's eyes fluttered open. Why had visions of Everard Ramsey popped into her head? 'Twas extremely disloyal and unflattering to Justin to be making these comparisons, though much as she adored Justin, she was obliged to admit the truth of her observations.

'Twas clearly Mr. Snape's fault if her thoughts were so jumbled. She would tell no one about what had happened here today. The man was a coward, full of bluster, his threats not to be taken seriously. In any case, if his affairs were as bad as 'twas rumored, the man would likely lose his lease on Wetherbee Hall and go back to London where he came from. She would not waste another moment's thought upon the horrid creature.

Chapter 3

Everard Ramsey padded across the thick Brussels carpet in his stocking feet, moving closer to the mahogany-framed cheval glass. In the soft glow of wax candles mounted on either side, the mirror reflected back his well-honed body, the lean musculature but scantily disguised by a pair of tight-fitting black Florentine silk breeches and an immaculate white frilled shirt. Bending forward, he began to fold the foot-long tie carefully around his collar. His deft fingers stayed momentarily as he paused to frown at the faint purplish mark lingering on his forehead, all that remained of the enormous goose egg he had sported from the curricle accident of a week ago. Mayhap, he thought with a wry grimace, when even this trace of the bruise disappeared, Justin would no longer plague him with jests about trying to set a new fashion for three-wheeled curricles.

His balding, dapper little valet, Beddoes, scurried about the large oak-paneled bedchamber, picking up the sweat-soaked breeches and shirt Everard had discarded earlier that afternoon after his attempt to teach the son of a local baronet some of the finer points of fencing. Beddoes gingerly reached for the blunted foil, whose steely length glinted brightly against the crimsom damask bedcover.

"Did you have good sport with young Master Winchell

today, sir?'' he asked as he replaced the light sword in its silk-lined case.

''Ummm,'' Everard replied, raising his chin. He had reached the critical stage of putting the creases into the starched linen cravat. 'Twas rumored that Beau Brummell, threw away scores of stocks before one was arranged to his taste. Everard scorned such a waste of time, when perfection could be achieved on the first effort with just a little concentration.

''There,'' he pronounced when the last fold of the *trône d'amour* stood out in pristine crispness against his shirt-front. ''Yes, the bout with Master Winchell went well enough,'' he replied. ''What the lad lacks in skill, he makes up for in enthusiasm. In any event, 'twas far more diverting than spending another day with Lord Spencer upon the river, watching him wreak havoc amongst the mallards.''

He wondered if that was how Justin had occupied himself, or if he had gone to call upon Miss Sinclair again, as Everard had suggested. Despite his badgering, Justin had only been to Sinclair Manor twice since the morning of the proposal. Not that it was any of his affair, but he was troubled by an image of Aurelia, standing by her window, day after day, her green eyes clouded as she regarded the empty stable yard below. Damn it, marriage of convenience or not, 'twas shabby indeed how Justin neglected the girl.

''I entirely agree with you, sir.''

''What?'' Startled, Everard wondered if he had been voicing his thoughts aloud, but Beddoes's next comment reassured him.

''About the hunting, sir. You always were too refined for such sport as only amuses the rustics.''

''Oh, that. No, I fear hunting mostly bores me because I am a notoriously bad shot.'' He raised his arms so that Beddoes could help him don a striped marcella waistcoat and jacket of black superfine. "Unlike Arthur, who could kill more birds than any other man in England."

"So your late brother was wont to say, sir." Beddoes gave a contemptuous sniff, then stepped back as Everard smoothed out the lapels. "Perfect, sir. What a pity it must be wasted at a dinner party given for a parcel of country bumpkins."

Everard's mouth tipped upward in amusement. "What a dreadful old snob you are, Beddoes. As it happens, this is a very special dinner party, given by my aunt to celebrate the betrothal of my best friend to a most charming lady. And whatever other social graces Aunt Lydia might lack, I assure you she sets a table to rival anything you would find in town."

Beddoes's brow crinkled, his upturned nose showing that he was singularly unimpressed. "And when, sir, if I might take the liberty of asking, will we be able to return to town?"

Everard's gaze shifted to a small Sheraton writing desk, its lacquered surface littered with thick white envelopes, duns that had followed him from London.

"Not anytime soon, I fear. In fact, you'd best brace yourself to spend the winter in exile."

"Oh, sir!"

"Unless, of course, you choose to abandon me here amongst the barbarians and seek service elsewhere. 'Tis always prudent, you know, to desert a sinking ship before the water gets too deep."

Beddoes eyed him reproachfully. "I shall not even dignify such a heartless jest with a reply, sir."

At that moment, a loud rap sounded on the bedchamber door. Everard winced. "That would be Aunt Lydia, wanting to know what the devil detains me so long. Beddoes, would you inform my aunt I shall be down directly?"

"Very good, sir," the valet said, expressing his still wounded feelings by the stiff set of his shoulders as he strode over to answer the door. After a brief exchange of murmured words, he returned bearing a large parcel.

" 'Twas not a message from your aunt, sir, but one of Lord Spencer's servants delivering this package from his lordship."

Everard glanced at it with mild surprise. "Well, open it."

But Beddoes handed the parcel to Everard, as if he feared it might explode. "If 'tis all the same to you, sir, I had much rather not."

Everard flung back his head and laughed, recalling Beddoes dismayed expression at the last parcel that had arrived from Justin: a most handsome dressing gown that the valet had held aloft with delight, only to recoil shrieking from the garter snake that tumbled from the silken folds, hissing its resentment of having its sleep disturbed. Still chuckling at Beddoes uneasiness, Everard tore off the brown paper, revealing a flat rectangular cherrywood case. He proceeded with extreme caution as he lifted the lid. With Justin, there was no telling. . . .

"What the deuce?" he exclaimed as he stared down at a pair of flintlock top-hammer pocket pistols, the handles inlaid with silver lions and blue steel.

Beddoes, who had been holding his breath, exhaled with relief. "Here is the note that accompanied it, sir."

Everard set the pistol case down upon the bed, then tore open the envelope. He grinned as he perused the first part of the letter.

> . . . thought you could use these to get in a little practice. Then, perchance, the next time we go hunting, there will be other wildlife, in mortal danger besides myself.

But as Everard scanned the rest of the page, his smile abruptly vanished.

Regret to say I will not be joining in the festivities this evening. Urgent affairs at my estate at Hoxley demand my immediate attention. I am setting out even as I write this to you. Don't know when I shall return. Look in on Reely for me from time to time.

Urgent affairs? Aye, but not at Hoxley, Everard would have wagered his life upon it. Hoxley was a small manor in the hands of an extremely capable bailiff. Its chief attraction was that it was quite near the country estate of Lady Sylvie Fitzhurst.

"Be damned to you, Justin." Everard crumpled the note and tossed it into the fireplace grate.

Beddoes coughed discreetly. "So Lord Spencer is plotting more of his mischief, is he, sir?"

"The mischief has already been accomplished."

Everard wondered what Miss Sinclair had said when Justin informed her of his plans. Of course, she would have no way of guessing the truth as to why her betrothed could not be troubled to attend a party given in honor of their engagement. She would only know that he was not to be there, that fact alone enough to cast a damper over her spirits, Everard was sure.

"Of all the inconsiderate young fools." He muttered to himself for several minutes in this vein before he realized Beddoes was waiting for him to finish venting his anger and don his freshly blackened Hessians.

"Do you believe this will be a late evening, sir?" the valet asked, warily stepping back as Everard snatched the boot from his grasp. "Shall I wait up?"

Everard jammed one foot inside the stiff leather. "No, Beddoes. Completely unnecessary. I greatly fear this is going to be a very short celebration."

Everard paused on the threshold of the cedar-paneled drawing room, the large, well-appointed chamber almost masculine in its starkness, the tall mullion-paned windows shorn of any draperies, the walls bare except for the occasional painting depicting the hunt. Aunt Lydia could not abide frills.

He raised his quizzing glass to study the company gathered about the fire crackling in the hearth, warding off the early autumn chill. In vain did he seek for the burnished tint of auburn hair, laughing emerald eyes. Aurelia had not yet arrived.

His gaze skimmed impatiently over the local gentry Lady Foxcliff had assembled for this evening's party: Justin's mother, Lady Spencer, the picture of stately elegance as always, her eldest married daughter, Clarice, looking enough like Justin to have been his twin, Clarice's stocky husband, Lord Norton. Grouped further away from the fire, Squire Morley wheezed a laugh at some jest of carrot-haired Winchell Denison; the vicar and his lady conversed earnestly with sundry others whose names Everard did not remember.

But doubtless Aurelia knew every last one of them well, these, the friends and neighbors she had grown up amongst, who would now bear witness to her humiliation this evening. Small wonder that she had not as yet put in an appearance. Most likely a note would arrive at any moment: "Miss Sinclair regrets, but she has been of a sudden taken ill." Everard lowered his glass, silently cursing Justin once more.

"Ha! So you've decided to grace us with your presence at last." The boisterous female voice, accompanied by a sharp jab in the ribs, caused Everard to jump. Rubbing his side, he turned to face his aunt's scowl. Garbed in a plain, straight gown of ecru satin straining across her strapping shoulders, her ladyship put Everard in mind of a tall marble pillar. Her iron-gray curls, done up in a profusion of sausage curls, bobbed with energy as she shook her finger at Everard.

"Confound it, sir, how could it take any man so long to rig himself out? Why, my third husband, Harry, God rest his soul, frequently dressed himself in less than five minutes."

"And frequently looked it, too." With a movement born from long experience, Everard quickly moved the knuckles of his right hand out of range of her ladyship's ivory-handled fan.

"Unlike yourself, dear Aunt," he continued smoothly, "who, as usual, quite puts all the other ladies into the shade this evening." He bent forward and planted a swift kiss upon one heavily rouged cheek.

"Flattering rogue." Balked of the knuckles, Lady Foxcliff dealt a forcible rap to Everard's shoulder, but he could see the trace of pink stealing along her square jawline.

His aunt lowered her voice to tones that were meant to be confidential, but were still quite loud enough for the entire room to hear.

"So, what do you think of this mad behavior of Justin's? Disgraceful, I call it. If I were the boy's mama, I should never have permitted him to go haring off to Hoxley."

"I am sure he wouldn't have, Aunt, without an—an excellent reason." Everard's lips tightened as he gave voice to the lie, but after all, Justin was his friend.

"Humph. Can't be any good reason for leaving Reely in the lurch, to say nothing of ruining my table arrangements. Now I've got one too many females." Her ladyship glared at her guests. "If I had only had some warning, I could have found a way to be rid of one of these dratted girls."

Lady Spencer and Clarice who were well accustomed to her ladyship's outspoken ways kept talking as if they had not heard, but Everard noted with amusement that the vicar's daughter paled with dismay.

"I shouldn't worry about your numbers, Aunt Lydia,"

he said softly. "For I very much doubt that Miss Sinclair will—"

He never had opportunity to complete the thought, for the door to the drawing room suddenly swung open and Lady Foxcliff's sour-faced butler thrust his head in to announce.

"Miss 'Relia Sinclair and Mrs. Perkins, yer ladyship."

As Aurelia stepped into the room, followed by her elderly companion, Everard became aware of a lull in the conversation behind him, but he could not tear his eyes away from Aurelia. She was garbed in another of those hideous dresses that accented all the worst points of her figure, this time one of dove-gray silk with so much lace and so many rosette trims, Everard longed to get after it with a pair of scissors. But she could have worn sackcloth for all the difference it made to the way she appeared tonight.

Green eyes dancing, a becoming flush in each cheek, she had entwined a single rose of pink silk in her luxuriant hair. Auburn curls flowed loose about her shoulders, the glow of fire playfully captured in each glossy strand. Why, she looks positively radiant, Everard thought with a bemused frown. Mayhap he was mistaken about her feelings for Justin. Surely, not even the most courageous of women could disguise her chagrin over her beloved's defection to that extent.

As if aware of his stare, her gaze swept up to meet his with that direct, honest regard so different from the missish way most females fluttered their eyes. 'Twas both delightful and disconcerting. Scarce thinking, he fumbled for his quizzing glass and wielded it before his eye like a jouster settling a protective shield into place.

"Good evening, Miss Sinclair."

Her chin came up a trifle as she raised a quizzing glass of her own. Her eyes twinkled at him like bright green jewels; her lips widened into a smile of impish challenge.

41

"And a very good evening to you, Mr. Ramsey." She rolled the syllables off her tongue in precise imitation of his own languid tones.

They stood for a long moment, eye to eye, unblinking until Everard's gravity was the first to break. He lowered his glass, no longer able to restrain his smile.

"Ah, Miss Sinclair, I see you have adopted my habit of employing a quizzing glass. So useful is it not, for locating small objects, such as—as a pair of scissors."

"Indeed, sir. Or even larger objects, such as a pony cart."

Everard choked, but before he could think of a proper retort, his aunt swooped in, enveloping Aurelia in a hug of exuberant welcome.

"Well, Reely, at least you can always be depended upon to do what's right and proper. Only fancy! Not attending one's own engagement party. Rag manners, I call it."

Aurelia's musical laughter rang out. "Oh, no. Don't tell me Justin is being fashionably late again."

At her words, an awkward silence descended over the guests. The damned scoundrel never told her he was going away, Everard thought as he watched Aurelia's smile waver, her brow furrow with uncertainty as her gaze swept the room.

"Hell's fire!" Lady Foxcliff bellowed, causing the vicar to wince. She glowered at Lady Spencer. "That harumscarum boy of yours has gone shabbing off to Hoxley and never breathed a word to Reely about it."

"I am sure *my son* left a note to be delivered," Lady Spencer replied in arctic accents. "One of the servants has obviously been grossly negligent."

"Stuff! You know right well Justin never did. He has always been an inconsiderate young brute. If I had my say in the matter, Reely would never have accepted his offer."

While the two women engaged in a heated dispute over Justin's conduct, Everard watched the color fade from Aurelia's cheeks, like a killing frost taking the bloom off a summer rose. The lashes lowered over her eyes concealing their expression. With a gesture that appeared almost unconscious, she reached up and plucked the pink flower from her hair.

Nervously twisting the silk petals between her fingers, Aurelia became aware of the averted eyes of most of the men, of the vicar's wife attempting to conceal her clucks of self-satisfied disapproval behind her fan. Aurelia shrugged, trying to smile, searching for the jest that wouldn't come.

Justin had ridden over twice to see her that week. Twice! she wanted to scream. He had stayed upward of half an hour, laughing and joking as if he truly enjoyed being with her, It had been like old times, when they had romped together as carefree children. The awkward manner of his proposal had been forgotten. Hope of winning his regard had been reborn.

She had dressed herself with such care for this evening, wanting to make him proud to claim her as his future bride, daring to let down her hair from the braids, even daring to fancy that she did look—oh, just a very little bit—pretty. Perhaps even the fastidious Mr. Ramsey would revise his poor opinion of her. She had smiled to herself, slipping the quizzing glass into her reticule, plotting her little jest to meet the man's challenging stare.

What a simpleton you are, she told herself scornfully. 'Tis not necessary for Justin to make a fool of you. You manage so wonderfully all on your own. Imagining yourself to be pretty when you know full well you are not. You don't deserve that Justin should care two pins about you.

She wished she could raise her head and laugh away all her neighbor's whispered comments about "Poor Reely" and their pitying glances. But her mouth felt so dry and she had a terrifying fear she was about to disgrace herself totally by bursting into tears.

At that moment, a cool male voice broke into Lady Spencer's rigid defense of her son against Lady Foxcliff's accusations.

"In truth, Justin's absence must be laid at my door." Lady Foxcliff and Justin's mama ceased their bickering long enough to stare at Everard Ramsey.

Aurelia's eyes flew to his impassive countenance, all her earlier suspicions against the man stirring to life once more.

"Yes," he continued, not batting so much as an eyelash, "I had Justin kidnapped by pirates to get him out of the way."

Lady Spencer looked considerably affronted, but amusement rippled amongst the other guests. Aurelia's chin came up. Was the man attempting to mock her and expecting that she would let him get away with it?

"Pirates, Mr. Ramsey?" she asked. "Here in Norfolk?"

"Actually, I had to import them from the Mediterranean, Miss Sinclair. Shockingly expensive business. Had to spout my watch to do it."

Lady Foxcliff let out a loud guffaw. Ramsey's air of casual nonchalance while rehearsing this outrageous tale caused even Lady Spencer's thin lips to curve reluctantly.

"You see, Miss Sinclair, I knew if I did not proceed to such extremes, I would not have a single hope of being able to partner you at dinner this evening. I trust I am to be rewarded for my pains?" Ramsey offered her his arm, one dark brow arched questioningly.

Aurelia eyed him for a moment, wondering what mischief lay behind this gallant gesture. His polite smile told her nothing. But his eyes . . . An unexpected spark of warmth appeared in the blue depths, not of pity, but of such an uncanny empathy with her feelings as caused a shiver to work its way up her spine.

She lowered her gaze in confusion, hesitating. Yet whatever the man's motives, she could not help feeling grateful for his intervention. His jest had relieved the tension, helped her to regain command of herself.

"I do not see how I can refuse you, Mr. Ramsey," she said. "I always believe ingenuity should be encouraged."

With all the dignity she could muster, she linked her arm through his. His hand came up to cover her fingers, which rested lightly against his jacket sleeve.

How strange, she thought. Strange that a gentleman as coolly elegant as Everard Ramsey should have a hand that felt so warm and strong.

As Effie nodded off on one of the drawing room chairs while waiting for the carriage to be brought round, the mantelpiece clock chimed quarter past midnight. Aurelia started at the sound, astonished that the evening had passed so quickly. She usually found these dinner parties such interminable affairs. What had been so different about this one?

Her attention strayed involuntarily toward Everard Ramsey. With great difficulty she snapped her head back, trying to concentrate upon what Justin's sister was saying.

". . . and I don't know why you wish to marry Justin, Reely." Clarice's pert nose crinkled. "He's the greatest beast in nature. But I am *so* glad you are going to be my sister."

"Clarice. The coach . . ." Her husband stood on the drawing room threshold, yawning and tapping his foot.

"I shall be there directly." Clarice bestowed upon Aurelia a farewell embrace, whispering in her ear, "And I have not even had opportunity to tell you the most exciting news. I am *enceinte*."

When Aurelia offered her delighted congratulations, Clarice gave a trill of laughter. "Only fancy. Soon I shall be as round and plump as—"

The girl broke off in confusion, blushing at her faux pas.

45

Although Aurelia winced, she gave Clarice a wry smile. Justin's sister had never been noted for her delicacy or tact.

After such a blunder, Lady Norton heeded her husband's demand to be gone with alacrity, only pausing long enough to assure Aurelia that she must be the babe's godmother. Clarice would have no one else. Aurelia's quiet acceptance was all but lost as the impatient Lord Norton fairly dragged his wife from the room.

With a deep sigh, Aurelia self-consciously smoothed the folds of her gray silk gown over her stomach, then turned toward the remaining guests. Sir Marcus and Lady Denison were having extreme difficulty tearing their eldest offspring away from his fascinating discourse with Everard Ramsey on fencing. Aurelia marveled at Ramsey's relaxed demeanor, so unlike his usual hauteur. He leaned against the mantel, a graceful negligence in his pose, the arrogant planes of his countenance softened by the light and shadow cast by the flickering flames.

She would have sworn it unthinkable that he would deign to waste his time upon a raw country lad, listening to the boy rattle on about hits, thrusts, and parries. Or that the elegant town beau would have gone out of his way to entertain her at dinner, keeping her on the verge of laughter with his anecdotes of the haut ton, until she had nigh forgotten her hurt over Justin's absence.

I believe I was mistaken about your friend, Justin, Aurelia thought. Given time, I might even learn to like him.

As if she had spoken aloud, Everard's eyes traveled in her direction. Aurelia quickly sank down upon a cherry-striped divan, behaving as if it were a manner of life-threatening urgency if she did not locate her handkerchief inside her reticule.

Lady Foxcliff bounded into the drawing room. Having just bade good-night to Clarice and Lord Norton, she now proceeded to gather up the Denisons. Forcibly pulling Winchell away from Everard, she said, "Well, well. So delightful having all of you here, but no point in wearing out one's welcome, is there?''

The young man scarce had time to make his farewells before her ladyship had propelled him after his parents out of the room.

"Dear me," Aurelia said, "I do hope Morrison has the horses in the traces, or I fear I shall find myself sitting out upon the drive."

Everard drew forth his watch and consulted it. "If your coachman does not bring your carriage round within the next five minutes, I have strict orders from Aunt Lydia to carry you out."

Aurelia joined in his laughter, but stopped when he crossed the room and sat down beside her. The room seemed to grow oddly quiet, except for the crackle of the fire and Effie's gentle snores from the opposite end of the parlor. Aurelia twisted the large ruby weighting down her hand, wondering why these attacks of shyness always beset her at the most awkward of moments.

"You appear to have made quite an impression on Winchell Denison," she said, striving to break the silence. "I believe I have never seen him in anything but buckskins and a frock coat. He was actually wearing a cravat tonight."

"Good Lord. Is that what it was? I feared I must have inadvertantly pinked the boy in the throat during our match earlier and his mama had swathed him in bandages."

She chuckled. "But indeed, it was very kind of you to spend your afternoon instructing Winchell, when I am sure there were other things you would much rather have done."

She felt him shrug, the movement causing his shoulders to brush up against hers. Aurelia fought down a blush, inching a little further away.

"I greatly enjoy a little exercise with the foils myself. Alas, it seems to be a dying art, one of the last traces of an age of elegance, before gunpowder came to dominate, with all its dirt and noise."

His voice took on a dreamy quality. "I've often wished I could have learned to wield a real sword, one of those heavy lengths of steel as the knights used to—"

He stopped suddenly. When Aurelia raised her head, daring to look at him, she was astonished to find Ramsey appearing a trifle sheepish, a hint of red darkening his cheeks. He muttered something about running on like a dead bore.

"Not at all, Mr. Ramsey. Do go on." He had disconcerted her so often in their brief acquaintance, she could not resist the opportunity of having some of her own back. "You were telling me you would like to be a knight, riding a white charger no doubt, rescuing damsels in distress."

"Certainly not," he snapped. "I never have the least patience with young ladies who attempt to introduce dragons into polite society."

"You need have no fears about me on that score. I always slay my own."

"Do you, indeed? A most perilous occupation. One runs such a danger of being scorched." His gaze took on that penetrating quality that Aurelia found so unsettling. She barely knew this man, harbored mixed feelings about him at best, and yet he seemed to slip past her barricades of feigned good humor with ease, wandering down the secret paths of her mind where she permitted entry to no one.

"Gracious. I wonder what is keeping my carriage." She fumbled for her reticule and attempted to rise, wanting only to escape those keen blue eyes that saw far too much, but Everard's strong fingers encircled her wrist.

"Aurelia."

Flustered, she tried to assume an expression of haughty reproach at his use of her name.

"Miss Sinclair," he continued, pausing as if weighing each word with care. "About Justin. Sometimes he can be such a heedless fellow. You ought to write and give him a good set-down for his blackguard behavior. 'Twill make you feel much better than if you simply smile and tolerate it.''

Aurelia stiffened at Ramsey's blunt criticism of her betrothed. What impertinence! That he should tell her how to deal with Justin, she, who had known Lord Spencer far longer than Ramsey ever had. She jerked her hand away, but she could still feel the disturbing warmth of Everard's touch banding her flesh.

"Justin has a perfect right to do as he likes," she said, "without being made to feel guilty."

Ramsey leaned back against the cushion, folding his arms across his chest. "The right to trample roughshod over your feelings, as though you were a cobblestone? Tell me, Miss Sinclair, do you never get angry with Justin? Do you always feel obliged to conceal your emotions, even from the man you love?"

Aurelia gasped, the color surging into her face. She drew her arms in closer to her bosom, feeling as exposed as if Everard had undone the ribbons of her chemise. Attempting to hide her embarrassment, she examined the lace cuff of her gown and said tartly, "How odd. I don't recall having worn my heart upon my sleeve tonight."

"You never do. I read the inscription in that book that fell out of your workbasket."

"Have you never heard of the word *privacy*, Mr. Ramsey? I have never advocated the practice of book burning before, but in future, I shan't be so liberal."

Completely unperturbed by her rebuke, Ramsey stroked his chin in thoughtful fashion. "I don't mean to offer advice where it may not be wanted, but you intrigue me, Miss Sinclair. You have from the first. If you could get past the point of letting Justin treat you with less consideration than he shows his horse, I believe you are exactly the sort of woman he needs."

49

"Well, I can't begin to tell you how much your opinion means to me, sir." Aurelia glowered, spanning her fingers along her waistline. "Such a nice, sensible, *solid* sort of woman, is that your estimation?"

"No," he retorted. "Such a lovely, intelligent woman who, for some strange reason, is at pains to hide her beauty behind a silken monstrosity that resembles a rose garden run amok."

"For your information, sir, this happens to be my best gown. And—and roses are my favorite flower." She shot to her feet, all her gratitude for his earlier rescue of her evaporating, her hearty dislike returning in full force. "I fear my appearance will never measure up to your *exacting standards*, Mr. Ramsey." She lowered her voice when Effie shifted on her chair, stirring in her sleep. "What with the shortage of magic wands of late, I shall never be transformed into the belle of the ton."

He also stood, but with a more leisurely grace. "You could be, if that is what you desire. All you need is the right tutor. Place yourself under my direction, and Justin would not be the only man you would dazzle with your charms. Indeed, he would have to mount guard to prevent your being snatched from his arms."

For a brief moment Aurelia was entranced by the picture Ramsey's words conjured before her eyes. How oft had she dreamed of promenading into a ballroom upon Justin's arm, her lithe figure swirled in a gossamer gown that was the envy of all the ladies, Justin darting jealous glances at the men, daring them to approach her.

But reason quickly intruded, in the sharp memory of her mother's voice echoing through her mind. Lady Sinclair had thrown up her hands as she watched Aurelia being garbed for her coming-out party, the corset strings not quite managing to pull tight enough. *God knows I've tried, Aurelia, but you will never be a beauty. You take after your father's side of the family, every one of them hopelessly fat. The most we can hope for is that you will learn not to be so awkward.*

"And the most we can hope for," Everard was saying, "is that not too many men will lose their lives fighting duels over you."

Aurelia gave her head a brief shake, dispelling the painful recollection of her mother, along with the rosy haze of her dreams.

"You'll need a different manner of dressing your hair," Ramsey continued. "And some new gowns cut upon straighter, more elegant lines."

"By all means," Aurelia said bitterly. "In case anyone has missed any of the flaws in my figure, let us be sure to accent them."

Ramsey stepped back a pace, studying her curves in expert, assessing fashion. Aurelia's cheeks burned. If he reaches for his quizzing glass, she thought, I'll break it over his nose.

But Everard appeared satisfied with his brief inspection. "No, 'tis not as desperate a case as you imagine it to be. Granted, you will want to trim off a few pounds."

Aurelia thought if she had not been so angry, she would have wept. What ungentlemanly insult would he utter next? Worst of all, he did not speak lightly, as though in jest.

"You must be bored, indeed, Mr. Ramsey. Have you such an urge to play Pygmalion, then?"

"If that is how it pleases you to describe my offer, Miss Sinclair."

"It doesn't please me at all. I am not a statue!"

"Well, who the devil said you were?" Lady Foxcliff bellowed from the doorway, causing Aurelia to jump. She stepped inside the room, scowling from Everard to Aurelia. "Now what has that nevvy of mine been saying to make your face come over all splotchy like that?"

"Nothing. Just a parcel of nonsense." Aurelia spun on

her heel and strode over to the Queen Anne chair. She shook Effie awake none too gently.

"Aurelia," Mrs. Perkins murmured sleepily. "Has the carriage come yet?"

"If it hasn't, we're walking home." Ignoring Effie's wail of dismay at her threat, Aurelia hauled her to her feet. Scarce giving the bewildered Mrs. Perkins time to don her cloak, she bundled her out to the waiting carriage.

After Effie was safely bestowed in the darkened interior, Aurelia felt Everard place his hand upon her elbow to help her up the coach steps.

"I am sorry if I've upset you, Miss Sinclair. But I don't take back a word I've said. My offer still stands. You could be as beautiful—"

Aurelia wrenched her arm away, nearly stumbling as she scrambled into the coach. She plopped down onto the squabs, thrusting her head forward for one last glare at Everard Ramsey. Moonlight skimmed his handsome face; his blue eyes were lit with the same brilliant intensity as the North Star. She could not tell if he was serious about this mad proposal or merely mocking her with some outrageous jest.

"Mr. Ramsey, I strongly suggest you go soak your head in a bucket of cold water. You have obviously had far too much champagne."

Not waiting for his reply, she pulled the coach door from his grasp, closing it in his face with a loud slam. Everard stepped back as the coach lumbered off down the gravel drive.

"Well, Ramsey," he said to himself with a rueful sigh. "You handled that with all the finesse of—of a Justin Spencer." Maybe Aurelia was right. Perhaps he *was* slightly foxed. What was he about, making such suggestions to her, meddling in what was obviously none of his concern?

He grunted as, the next instant, his aunt gave him a sharp poke in the back.

"Now, sir. I have never seen Reely in such a taking in all her days, and I've known that girl from the cradle. What was that flummery I heard you a-whispering to her about being beautiful?"

"I made her an offer which she found rather unpalatable."

"An offer, you rogue! You know perfectly well she's engaged to that scamp, Justin Spencer, more's the pity."

"Not that sort of an offer, Aunt." Cursing himself for a blundering fool, Everard started to kick the toe of his boot into the gravel, then stopped. Beddoes would faint in horror if he scuffed the Hessians. When Lady Foxcliff continued to hector him, he explained reluctantly, "I offered her my help in altering her appearance. Aurelia could be a diamond of the first water if she chose to be."

Lady Foxcliff scowled. "You've got maggots in your brain, lad. Why, Reely's a good, sensible girl, the best, in my opinion, but as for beauty—pshaw. I've always had a face that would rival anything in my stables, but I've done just fine, thank you—seen three husbands to their graves."

Although Everard laughed, he immediately sobered. "Aye, but 'tis different for Aurelia, Aunt Lydia. She seems to hold herself in such low esteem."

" 'Tis the fault of that mother of hers. Nasty, disparaging tongue Clarabelle Sinclair had. But you won't help poor Reely's esteem a jot by filling her head full of crack-brained notions. Can't make silk out of sackcloth."

Everard felt a twinge of impatience. He was beginning to find all these comments about Aurelia's plainness as irritating as his father's constant references to Arthur's many virtues. "I tell you, Aunt, Aurelia could outshine any woman in England. I would wager a thousand pounds, I could change her—"

"Done!" the old lady shouted, slapping her thigh.

"I could teach her to—I—I beg your pardon?" Everard asked startled.

"I said, 'Done.' I accept your wager."

"Aunt Lydia"—Everard chuckled uncertainly.— " 'Twas only a figure of speech."

"What, sir! Are you trying to weasel out of the wager already? And you, with your reputation of being such a reckless gamester!"

Everard eyed her with suspicion. "If this is your way of trying to give me money yet again, Aunt Lydia, I warn you, I won't have it."

"Hoity-toity," her ladyship blustered. " 'Tis you who will end by paying me. You will never win this bet, my lad. Especially considering the look Reely gave you when she slammed that carriage door. Appeared as if she was imagining she had your head caught in the opening. She'll have nothing to do with your schemes."

"Ah, but she will, Auntie. When I desire, I do possess a certain amount of address with the ladies."

"Conceited rogue. Well, we shall see. But I think you've met your match in Reely. Too stubborn by half." With a resounding buffet to his ribs, Lady Foxcliff made her way back into the red brick Georgian mansion, still clucking her tongue at him.

Grimacing, Everard rubbed his side. Leaning against one of the portico's towering white pillars, he took a deep breath. Although he had no intention of accepting his aunt's wager, he could not allow such a challenge to go unanswered. Aurelia Sinclair, sackcloth? He would show Aunt Lydia what a pearl lay hidden beneath the shell. And Justin, too.

Justin. Everard's mouth split into a grim smile as the thought came to him. Aye, a way to settle a few scores for the snake, the pepper, the bit of muslin slipped into his bed. He would see Justin properly dished this time. Not only would he turn Aurelia into a beauty, but he would make Justin fall helplessly in love with her as well.

Everard's sudden bark of laughter split the still night air.

Chapter 4

A glum silence settled over the breakfast table, broken only by the clatter of forks against the china. Aurelia stared out the bay front window, the brightness of the yellow chintz curtains and the snowbound world beyond dazzling her eyes.

She blinked, shifting her gaze toward Everard's plate, heaped with pressed beef, ham, cold tongue, and then to Effie, munching a muffin dripping with marmalade and honey butter. The tiny woman paused to lick a stray drop of honey from her fingertip in a gesture that was pure torture to Aurelia. Her stomach emitted an angry rumble. Small wonder, when the last time she could remember enjoying a meal of any substance was the night of Lady Foxcliff's dinner party several months ago.

She shoved away her glass of vinegar-and-water, wondering for the thousandth time why she had ever permitted Everard to cajole her into this madness. The day after the engagement party, she'd thought that he had ridden to Sinclair Manor to apologize for his insults. Instead, the man had alternately coaxed and bullied her, attempting to convince her to cooperate with his absurd scheme, flinging out the barb that he supposed she lacked bottom. After all, it took a certain amount of courage to make sweeping changes in one's life. Of course, if winning Justin's devotion was not important enough for her to be bothered . . .

Damn Everard Ramsey! How well the rogue knew where to find the chinks in her armor. But why was he at such pains to do so? She studied his profile as he slowly chewed the last bite of ham. He was, ever, point-device; the frothy folds of his cravat spilled across his navy jacket, and the only thing out of place was one stubborn dark curl that drooped over his forehead.

The man was still an enigma to her. So cool, so meticulous, he looked nothing like the reckless gamester he was reputed to be, wildly flinging his fortune away at hazard, hiding in Norfolk to escape his creditors. He behaved as if he had not a worry in the world, as if nothing were more important to him than trying to turn a dowdy country-bred female into a fashionable beauty.

Boredom, she supposed, could drive a man into doing some peculiar things. And yet, there was not a trace of ennui in the twinkling blue eyes that now looked up at her.

Everard slid her glass back into place, favoring her with a teasing smile. "Eat your breakfast, Aurelia. There's a good girl."

She glared first down at her plate of rice and then at him. "I refuse to eat another mouthful of this detestable stuff. This is pure madness. I don't know why I permit you to torment me in this fashion."

"Because, occasionally, there are moments when you forget yourself and lapse into bouts of being sensible." He patted her arm.

"Don't touch me in that condescending fashion," she said, the sour taste of vinegar lingering upon her tongue. "I'll bite your hand, I swear I will. That is how hungry I am."

"Tush." Everard leaned back in his chair and applied his napkin to his lips with a satisfied smile. "Your diet is more than adequate. Rice and vinegar. 'Twas what Lord Byron ate, and it did wonders for him.''

"Lord Byron is a fool. I shall never read *Childe Harold* again.''

Effie piped up, "I entirely agree. 'Tis all very well for poets to do such odd things. One expects them to be a little eccentric, but Aurelia is a lady of quality.''

She stood up and flounced to the sideboard, pouring out a steaming cup of chocolate. Balancing the delicate saucer and cup in one hand, she extended the dark, creamy brew to Aurelia. "Here, my dear, before you waste away entirely. Ring for Giddings and have that dreadful vinegar mess cleared away.''

Aurelia drew in a deep breath, her nostrils assailed by the rich aroma of chocolate. Her mouth watered as she reached for the cup, but before she could raise it to her lips, Everard snatched the china from her grasp.

"We'll have none of that,'' he said sternly, returning the chocolate to the sideboard. Aurelia moaned, her nails digging into the white linen tablecloth.

"Well, really, sir!'' Effie sputtered. She squared off with Everard, her quivering chin not quite reaching as high as the lacy edge of his starched cravat. Ramsey's narrowed eyes glinted down at her with the tolerant amusement of a great dark-winged falcon being twittered at by a small brown wren.

"This state of affairs cannot continue. Aurelia's dear papa would never have approved. Always, I remember how he worried that she did not eat enough, so afraid that she would tend to be of a consumptive nature, like many of her mama's sisters.''

"I think it highly improbable that Aurelia will develop consumption,'' Everard said.

"No, I am more like to die of starvation first.'' Aurelia poked her fork at the clumps of rice upon her dish, pulling a face at the sight of the tasteless grain. "And what do I have to show for it? I look as much a fright as I ever did."

"That is because you still dress as if you were a display of wares in a mantua maker's shop window. But after the new clothes that I ordered from London arrive—"

"Mr. Ramsey!" Effie's outraged gasp stopped him in midsentence. "Indeed, you have far exceeded the bounds of propriety this time."

"I fear I am forced to agree with her, Everard." Aurelia felt a blush coursing into her cheeks. "For you to be buying me clothes as if I were your—your . . ."

"My mistress?" he supplied, raising one eyebrow mockingly. "I assure you my finances are not in a state as to buy so much as a hatpin for a lady, even if I were so inclined."

Aurelia thought she detected a certain edge of bitterness in his voice, but it vanished as he continued, "No, ladies, rest assured all purchases were handled by my sister Philippa with great discretion. The demand for payment will be forthcoming."

Aurelia lowered her eyes, still fidgeting with embarrassment. "You might have consulted me first. I do have my own dressmaker."

"Ah, yes, that half-blind woman from the village who overstocked herself with lace and furbelows."

Aurelia's hand flew to the frills of her lime-green morning gown, the stiff ruffles of the high-necked gown scratching her chin. She wished she could think of a scathing retort to Everard's criticism, but 'twas impossible, when she knew he was right. Her wardrobe was woefully inadequate, especially considering that Justin, in one of his rare communications, had decided they should be married in London. Despite the fact Justin had implored her to name the day that would *make him the happiest of men*, he had set their wedding date himself. Late winter, nay, perhaps spring would be better. Then he would fetch Aurelia, and they could be wed at the fashionable St. George's in Hanover Square. The very thought of such a thing made Aurelia's stomach turn flip-flops.

"Excuse me, Aurelia." She felt Effie tug on her sleeve. Glancing up, she saw that Mrs. Perkins had gone as rigid as the fireplace poker, her lips pursed into a tight white line. "I wonder if I might have the favor of a few words in private, my dear?"

Aurelia sighed. She was in no humor for more of Effie's scolds, but she supposed 'twould be far less mortifying than having the woman rant on in Everard's hearing. Whisking the napkin off her lap, she flung it down by her place setting. "If you will excuse us a moment," she said to Everard.

He sketched her an exaggerated bow, his cool blue eyes impassive as he watched her follow Effie from the room.

Scarce able to contain herself, the little woman rounded on Aurelia as soon as they had crossed the threshold, not even bothering to pull the breakfast parlor door all the way closed.

"This madness has got to stop, Aurelia. 'Tis simply not proper! Bad enough to allow Mr. Ramsey to call upon you nigh every day, with Lord Spencer still away at Hoxley. I am supposed to be your chaperon. I shall be blamed if—"

"Now, Effie," Aurelia broke in soothingly. "I am scarce ever alone with Everard. And he is Justin's closest friend."

"That is another thing," Effie moaned. "What if anyone hears you calling him *Everard*!"

Aurelia caught a glimpse of Everard through the crack in the door, refilling her vinegar glass. "I daresay I shall be calling him much worse than that before this winter is over."

Effie squeezed Aurelia's hand in a distracted manner. "You are such an innocent, my dear. You cannot imagine how people might misconstrue. A single, personable man to be so often at the side of an unmarried lady—and so early in the day, too. At breakfast!''

Aurelia stiffened. ''If you are implying that Everard would ever behave in anything less than an honorable—''

''No, no.'' Effie hastened to disclaim. ''I am very fond of Mr. Ramsey myself. The dear boy! He is all that a gentleman ought to be. I realize he simply means to be kind. There is not the least fear that a man so fastidious would find *you* attractive.''

''No, he wouldn't would he?'' Aurelia fixed a wooden smile upon her lips. ''So, why make such a fuss?''

''Because of what others will say. The vicar's wife has already most kindly informed me there has been some gossip in the village.'' Effie's spiderlike hands fluttered to her cheeks. ''Oh, dear, and what if Lord Spencer got to hear of it? How dreadful 'twould be if he were to call Mr. Ramsey out and—and—''

''You have been reading too many Minerva Press novels again, Effie. Since Justin never troubles himself to return to Aldgate, he is unlikely to hear anything. And when he does''—Aurelia thrust out her chin proudly.—''I trust he will have more sense than to pay heed to the blathering of narrowed-minded individuals who twist an innocent friendship into something sordid.''

With that, she spun on her heel and stormed back into the breakfast parlor without waiting to see if Effie would follow her. She plunked back down in her seat, attacking the rice with her fork. She could sense that Everard was regarding her with a puzzled frown, but refused to meet his gaze until he lightly touched her hand.

''Aurelia, if I have offended you in the matter of the wardrobe, I am sorry. I thought you had given me carte blanche to do whatever I felt was necessary.''

''Y-yes, I did.'' She snatched her hand away as if he had scorched her, heat creeping into her cheeks. Plague take the vicar's wife, with her nasty, gossiping tongue, and plague take Effie for listening to her. Aurelia hadn't realized until this moment how comfortable she had become with Everard. Effie's insinuations somehow threatened the understanding that had sprung up between them, making Aurelia acutely aware of Everard's undeniable masculinity beneath the frilled shirts and elegantly cut waistcoats.

She squared her shoulders, straightening in her seat. Such foolish notions could entirely ruin their friendship if she let them. Well, she would not!

"Do not pay the least heed to me," she said with forced gaiety. "The vinegar has soured my disposition this morning. And I am nigh distracted, wondering what new horrors you have in store for me today. No more of those long trudges through the snow, I trust?"

"I would remind you, Miss Sinclair, that I was with you every step of the way, trudging, as you call it."

"Yes, but the freezing temperatures have not the same effect upon someone who has ice-water in his veins."

Everard withdrew the hand that she had shrunk from touching, his expression becoming more withdrawn as well. "I may not be as impervious to the cold as you think," he muttered. Some dark thought appeared to cloud his brow for a moment. Then, as if giving himself a shake, he said in lighter tones, "This afternoon, I propose we have our exercise indoors. 'Tis high time I taught you the proper manner to waltz."

Aurelia felt her muscles tense. The last time she had danced had been at the assembly, with Augustus Snape, when she had been so desperately tired of sitting against the wall. And look what that had brought down upon her head. At least, the dreadful man had finally left Norfolk and returned to London. But stumbling all over Mr. Snape's toes was entirely another matter. She had not the least desire to demonstrate to Everard how clumsy she was.

"I don't see how that will be possible," she said. "Unless you propose to hum while we dance."

"Mrs. Perkins will play for us."

Aurelia's gaze traveled the length of the table to Effie's empty chair. "I rather doubt that."

"Because she was a trifle vexed with me this morning?" Everard asked. "I think I can manage to bring her around." His lips twitched, but whether out of amusement or annoyance, Aurelia could not tell.

"Believe it or not, Miss Sinclair. There are a few women who occasionally are susceptible to my charms."

"I daresay," she retorted. "The same as there are women who are extremely susceptible to influenza. However, Effie's constitution may prove tougher than you imagine."

In truth, Aurelia was very much counting upon Elfreda's noted stubbornness to spare her a most uncomfortable and embarrassing exercise. But later, after she returned from consulting with her cook about the day's menu, Aurelia was taken aback to discover Mrs. Perkins and Everard already in the music room, moving back the furniture.

"Oh, good. There you are, Aurelia." Effie clapped her hands together, beaming at Aurelia as if she recalled not a word of their disagreement, nor any of the dire warnings she had issued only an hour ago. "Now we may begin."

Aurelia watched with dismay as Effie skittered over to the pianoforte, arranging her black silk skirts upon the bench. Everard stole a glance at Aurelia, then brushed his nails against his lapel, looking so smugly triumphant, Aurelia longed to shy her workbasket at his head.

He bent over Effie, helping her settle the music into place. " 'Tis prodigiously kind of you, Mrs. Perkins," he said in low, intimate tones. "And such a treat for us. 'Tis not often we are privileged to enjoy your musical talents."

As Effie preened and simpered, Aurelia thought she was going to choke. But why should she be so astonished when Aurelia knew how easy it was to find one's common sense floundering in the treacherous depths of those dark-fringed blue eyes?

Desperately, Aurelia made one last effort to extricate herself from the ordeal to come. "Effie does play beautifully," she said. "What a pity the waltz is not yet danced in Aldgate, and she does not know how to play—"

"Pooh! I have not allowed myself to become as out of date as *some*." Effie began to pound out the three-quarter time of the waltz with the ease of long familiarity.

Aurelia shrank back as Everard advanced upon her with long purposeful strides. Ruefully, she stared down at his gleaming Hessians. Well, 'twas his own fault. The man deserved every scuff mark he was going to get.

"Give me your hand, Aurelia," Everard commanded.

Trembling, she permitted him to take her fingers within the warmth of his grasp. He positioned her other hand so that it rested lightly against his shoulder. Aurelia held herself rigid, standing nigh an arm's length away.

"Relax, Aurelia," he said, "You look as though you were about to visit the tooth drawer."

Her answering retort broke off with a gasp as his strong arm encircled her waist, pulling her so near she feared he must hear the thudding of her heart. Heat rose into her cheeks as she glanced at Effie, half hoping, half fearing her chaperon would intervene. But Mrs. Perkins only nodded in encouragement before beginning to bounce up and down, completely absorbed in her music.

Aurelia scarce comprehended Everard's instructions regarding the movement of her feet. She had never been this close to any man except her father. Why, Everard might as well have been embracing her. Snatches of her conversation with Effie drifted back into Aurelia's head . . . *A single personable man . . . no fear Mr. Ramsey would find you attractive . . . if Justin got to hear of it . . .*

As Everard attempted to whirl her in a circle, she stumbled forward, brushing against the hard plane of his chest.

"Are you all right?" he asked, tightening his arm about her waist.

She nodded, trying to extricate herself. "I knew this would be of no avail. I simply have no sense of rhythm."

He gave her an impatient shake. "Nonsense. You haven't even tried. Now start again and count this time. One-two-three. One-two-three."

Aurelia sighed, making a weak attempt to assimilate all his rapidly barked instructions. "Turn, Aurelia, and for pity's sake, smile. 'Tis customary, you know, to hold some conversation with your partner while dancing."

"I cannot count and talk at the same time."

"And, 'twill be considered excessively odd if you address all your remarks to your partner's waistcoat."

Goaded past endurance, Aurelia's head jerked up, but she realized it was a grave mistake. The fine carved lines of Everard's face hovered but inches from hers, his sensitive mouth quirked into that mocking half smile that was so peculiarly his own.

"Stop holding yourself so stiff. Anyone would think you had never danced with a man before."

"I assure you, sir, I have trod upon far more handsome—I mean—far better—feet than yours."

Everard's deep chuckle rumbled close to her ear. She fancied that she could feel his breath fanning the tendrils of hair along her brow. Ducking her head, Aurelia missed her footing, tramping down hard upon his instep.

Although she heard him suck in his breath, he made no comment upon her awkwardness. Yet her cheeks burned all the same.

Hopeless, she thought, her lashes batting aside the tears gathering in her eyes. Utterly hopeless, but Everard would never release her until she forced him to acknowledge the fact she was naught but a galloping clodpole.

Determined to show him how clumsy she could be, Aurelia gave over all effort to mind her steps, throwing herself into the waltz with a fierce abandon. The tempo of Effie's enthusiastic thumps along the keyboard struck an answering chord somewhere within Aurelia's angry jumble of emotions.

Strangely enough, instead of tripping headlong as she expected, Aurelia found she was moving in perfect harmony with every sway of Everard's polished steps.

"Much better," he said, his lips close to her ear.

As they glided past the piano, Aurelia heard Effie exclaim, "Why, Reely, how quickly you've caught on. I declare I've never seen you dance half so well."

Me? Dance well? Aurelia's startled thought echoed. But indeed she was. She could feel the rightness of her movements in every fiber of her body. Everard's touch became provocatively light now, the fingers skimming her waist, no longer tugging but gently waltzing her the length of the music room.

Waltzing? Nay, 'twas more like floating on air, swirling like a fragile autumn leaf caught in the throes of a powerful wind. An excited wave of merriment bubbled inside of Aurelia. Never before had she felt so light upon her feet, so graceful, so lithesome. When Everard led her into a series of twirls, her senses reeled from the sheer pleasure of it, headier than sipping champagne. The pianoforte, the fireplace, the French windows, all spun before her gaze, until her world had only one focus, Everard's deep blue eyes. Even when she began to stagger, she would not permit him to stop, until he nigh lost his own balance.

Panting with laughter, Everard tried to collapse back upon the settee, but Aurelia seized him by both hands, tugging insistently.

"No. Can't stop now," she gasped. "Just getting the feel of it. Effie, keep playing."

Everard permitted Aurelia to drag him back to the center of the room. "Very well," he cried in mock dismay. "But more slowly this time. A little decorum, if you please. I'd look no end a fool if I sprained an ankle dancing.''

Giggling like a schoolgirl, she slipped back into his embrace. It took a few moments for her to calm herself enough to catch the rhythm. But by the time they had gone down the room, she moved in perfect step with him, gliding as if she had waltzed with Everard Ramsey every night of her life.

She peered up at him, almost shyly. ''I—I can scarce believe it. You can't possibly know how clumsy . . . my mother always despaired that—I mean I never . . .'' She floundered, at a complete loss for words to express the wonder she was feeling.

But it was unnecessary. The warm light in his eyes told her that he knew, although he only smiled and said, ''Mayhap you simply never had the right partner.''

''Mayhap not,'' she said slowly. ''Or mayhap you do have a magical wand about you after all.''

When he laughed, it suddenly occurred to her how very much she *liked* Everard Ramsey this way, the cynical lines of his face relaxing, gentled by his smile. No bored mask of indifference, no elegant dandy hiding behind his quizzing glass. Simply a man who looked at her as if—

Aurelia's breath caught in her throat. As if it mattered naught whether she were beautiful. Because 'twas enough that he made her feel as if she were.

Dimly, Aurelia became aware of Effie's excited applause. The woman called out. ''Oh, you do waltz beautifully, my dear. 'Tis nothing short of a miracle. Why, Mr. Ramsey ought to be a dancing master.''

''Aye,'' Aurelia laughed happily. ''Only fancy how astonished Justin is going to be.''

She felt the arm encircling her waist stiffen. Everard jerked her to an abrupt halt. A strange expression crossed his features, an expression Aurelia could only describe as being like that of one slumbering, deep in dreams, being startled awake.

Before she could ask what was wrong, Everard released her, averting his gaze toward the fire. When he looked back at Aurelia again, he had schooled his features into their customary languid expression.

"Shall I play a cotillion now, Mr. Ramsey?" Effie asked eagerly. "Aurelia has always had difficulty with that."

"No," he said. "I believe I have had quite enough exercise for one day. Mayhap another time."

"Y-yes," Aurelia stammered, twisting her betrothal ring, wondering miserably what she had done to break the spell. An image of how she must have looked to Everard surfaced in her mind. A plain, awkward, ungainly female prancing about, tossing her head, imagining herself some sort of a fairy-tale princess. She must have appeared a complete fool. Her face flushed as she said stiffly, "Mr. Ramsey, I do want to—to thank you for the lesson and for spending so much time—"

He started to reach for her hand, then stopped. "Not at all, my dear," he drawled. "What else is there for one to do in this wilderness?"

His words cut her like the lash of a whip. Hurt and confused, she retreated to the fireside, rubbing her arms, feeling chilled, as if the French doors had blown open, letting in the icy blast of winter. She scarce heard his murmured words of farewell to Effie, or the door click as he let himself out.

Chapter 5

Aurelia picked her way through the collection of trunks and bandboxes, resisting the urge to kick pettishly aside one containing a bonnet of green silk trimmed with lilac ribbon. With these constant reminders of her imminent departure for London cluttering her bedchamber, she was beginning to feel much like a watch with its spring wound too tight.

Effie's coos of delight as she lifted the elegant bonnet from its wrapping only further served to irritate Aurelia. Defiantly, she picked up her oldest broad-brimmed hat of straw, decorated with some rather wilted looking cloth flowers, and rammed it on her head.

Effie didn't appear to notice, so engrossed was she in the packages from London. "Oh, doesn't Mr. Ramsey's sister have the most exquisite taste!" she exclaimed. "I have been longing to tell him I was quite mistaken about the new wardrobe. 'Twas really an excellent notion. Why do you suppose he did not call again yesterday?"

"I haven't the slightest notion," Aurelia said, loath to admit she had been wondering the same thing herself. Everard had been so aloof since that long-ago winter afternoon he had taught her to waltz. When she chanced to meet him in the village or at Lady Foxcliff's manor, he seemed determined to keep her at bay with cynical glances through his quizzing glass, his lips set in an infuriating attitude of detached boredom. It had become a challenge to break through his cool demeanor, set him laughing, but whenever she succeeded, he appeared excessively vexed with her.

Shoving a dressing case aside, Aurelia plopped down upon the downy quilt coverlet spread across her bed and tried to put all thoughts of Everard from her mind, but 'twas exceedingly difficult, when Effie persisted in talking about the man.

"I daresay Mr. Ramsey will call today, dear," Mrs. Perkins twittered as she began to refold the frothy layers of a new petticoat she had been examining. "He knows how very anxious you are getting about the journey to London."

Anxious? Aurelia grimaced. She was petrified at the notion of confronting Justin again in the midst of all his elegant tonnish friends. She hunched her shoulders in an effort to appear indifferent, to both the grim prospect lying before her and Everard's unexplained defection.

"I daresay Mr. Ramsey has found other far more amusing diversions than trying to starve me to death. In any case, you should be pleased." She glowered at Effie. "You were always complaining that he called too often."

"Yes, but I never meant he should stay away altogether." Effie regarded her with reproachful surprise. "Really, Aurelia. How you do take one up. You have been cross as crabs of late. Most unlike yourself."

Aurelia drew in a deep breath, knowing Effie's criticism was fully justified. She had felt strange these past days, alternating between the desire to burst into tears and the urge to smash something. "I—I am sorry if I have been snappish, Effie," she said. "I expect I am light-headed from want of food."

"But the diet has done wonders. That old gray frock of yours positively hangs on you. I thought you were going to give it to the kitchen maid."

"Sally didn't want it." Aurelia self-consciously patted the folds of her comfortable old serge gown.

"And you haven't even tried on any of your lovely new things." Effie held aloft an enchanting high-waisted morning gown done up in a dusky shade of primrose. "Pray, Aurelia, do try at least this one."

Feeling slightly ashamed of her ill humor, Aurelia reluctantly took the gown from Effie. Holding the gauzy lengths in front of her plain gray dress, she stalked over to regard herself in the bedchamber's only mirror, a small gilt-framed oval. She could detect no changes in herself whatsoever from the unattractive woman Justin had blithely bade farewell to last autumn. Mayhap, she was a trifle paler, that was all. And the frolicsome pink of the gown only seemed to accent the dark shadows under her eyes.

With its daringly low décolletage and bright embroidered hem, it would not permit her to blend into the woodwork as she had always managed to do in the past. She tried to imagine how Justin would react when he saw her wearing it, but 'twas difficult to bring into focus the image of his teasing, light gray eyes. Instead, the vision of cool blue ones set beneath mockingly arched dark brows kept intruding upon her thoughts.

"Given the right tutor, you could dazzle the ton next spring, be as beautiful as you desire," Everard had said. Had he ever believed that? It scarce mattered for 'twas obvious that he no longer did. Aurelia could place no other interpretation upon his continued absence. He had given up on her.

Well, she had always known she was a hopeless case. Why did it hurt so much more now that Everard apparently thought so, too? Aurelia dropped the pink gown back into the trunk.

"I haven't any more time for this nonsense, Effie," she said. "I have to pay a call upon one of the tenants before tea."

"But I thought you would wish to change. All these pretty new gowns to choose from." Effie's eyes rounded in horror. "Surely you don't intend to go calling in that hideous old gray sack."

"Old Mrs. McGinty will not care how I look, so long as I am bringing a basketful of her favorite jam."

Before Effie could protest any further, Aurelia seized her drab brown merino cloak and hurried from the room. She longed to escape from the sight of the elegant new clothes that only served to remind her of her own shortcomings, her sense of failure.

Mrs. McGinty's reed-thatched cottage nestled at the very edge of the Sinclair estate, only yards from one of the broads, those clear-water lakes that dotted the Norfolk landscape. In the distance brown-sailed wherries skimmed the silver surface like playful, daring birds defying the whitecaps that threatened to toss them off-balance.

The last of the winter snows had melted, leaving the lakeside path a veritable sea of coffee-colored mud. Yet Aurelia would have enjoyed the walk under other circumstances. As it was, she kept remembering the last time she had passed this way, Everard tugging on her hand, forcing her to keep up with his brisk pace, laughingly threatening that if she did not cease her grumbles about being hungry, he would chip a hole in the ice and catch an eel for her supper.

Huddling deeper into the folds of her brown cloak, she tipped forward the brim of her battered straw bonnet, shielding her face from the nip of the March wind. She supposed in future she would take all her walks alone. Wandering by the lakeside was not a diversion that would ever appeal to Justin.

Despite the mud, the roads were now quite passable. There was not the slightest reason in the world why Justin could not return to Aldgate and fetch her to London himself instead of waiting for Lady Foxcliff to bring her. Not the slightest, except for the myriad of reasons Justin manufactured in his infrequent letters. The tone of his writing oft reminded Aurelia of a young man trying to avoid having to escort his sister to a ball.

His sister. Of a sudden, Everard Ramsey's well-modulated voice echoed through her mind. *If Justin thinks of you as his sister, 'tis your own fault for never attempting to show him otherwise. But we are going to change all that.*

Why had she ever listened to him? She was far too old to believe in fairy tales.

Listlessly, Aurelia knocked at the cottage door, hoping to keep the visit short, but as usual, it was difficult to escape from the garrulous Mrs. McGinty. The old woman was suffering from a bout of rheumatism again, but that hadn't kept her from her baking, nor from pressing a large chunk of gingerbread upon Aurelia when she finally took her leave. As soon as she was out of sight of the cottage's whitewashed walls, Aurelia stared down at the tantalizing bit of cake fashioned in the shape of a lopsided little man, still warm from the oven. She supposed she could take it home to Effie for tea. But the pale sun had already shifted lower in the sky, casting long afternoon shadows across the shore of the reed-choked lake. By this time, Effie had most likely already stuffed herself with biscuits.

The spicy aroma of gingerbread wafted to her nostrils, warring for dominance over the loamy scent of the mud-washed earth. Aurelia's fingers inched the cake toward her mouth. The sly currant grin of the gingerbread man seemed to mock her as if taunting, "What would Everard say if he caught you thus?" As if it mattered what scathing remark he would utter, Aurelia thought bitterly. No one truly cared how plump she was, not Justin and certainly not Everard Ramsey. In a gesture of defiance, she bit off the gingerbread man's leg.

She chewed slowly, savoring each mouthful with a sense

of hollow satisfaction. But before she could take another bite, she was distracted by the sight of a punt making its way toward shore. From beneath the shade of her bonnet brim, she studied the tall man so expertly maneuvering his small craft. 'Twas not one of the cottagers. Even from this distance, she remarked the elegant cut of his trousers, the white shirt shoved up past the elbows, exposing the sinewy muscles of his forearms. He braced his powerful legs beneath him like some bold pirate captain surveying the deck of his ship, while midnight strands of hair whipped across his brow as he shaded his eyes, squinting in her direction.

Aurelia blinked, scarce trusting her vision. No, it could not possibly be!

"The devil," she exclaimed in dismay. What perverse mischance had brought Everard to this very spot, engaged in such an unlikely occupation? She whipped the gingerbread behind her back, entirely forgetting she had just sworn that she did not give a groat for Ramsey's opinion. Stepping backward, she attempted to slink into the line of willow trees, but 'twas already too late. Ramsey raised his hand, calling out her name.

She froze while he poled in to the side, distractedly seeking some way to rid herself of the gingerbread man. She thought of flinging it into the broad. No, Everard would be bound to notice. She ended by slipping the cake figure back into her pocket. Adjusting her bonnet to conceal the guilty flush mounting into her cheeks, Aurelia watched Everard leap to the bank with an athletic grace quite different from his usual languid movements. Proceeding to moor his craft to a low hanging branch of a slender birch, he deftly knotted the rope with the ease of long practice. He lifted a frock coat from the seat of the punt and slung it carelessly over his arm, as usual appearing entirely impervious to the elements.

Aurelia tried not to gape at him as he strode toward her, but 'twas the first time she had ever seen Everard appear

73

other than the picture of polished elegance. Despite his recent exertions, not so much as a speck of dirt marred his whipcord breeches, nor one wrinkle the folds of his plain, buff-colored waistcoat. But he wore no cravat; the top buttons of his shirt were undone to expose the vee of his chest. Aurelia caught herself staring in fascination at the dark hairs curling against the tanned flesh, then blushed more deeply than ever.

"Good afternoon, Miss Sinclair." He bowed with as much aplomb as though greeting her in the manor's most formal dining room.

She placed her fingers instinctively over the area of her cloak where the gingerbread nestled in her pocket. "Oh-h, Everard. How astonishing to meet you here. So unexpected. I would never have imagined that you . . ."

"That I could manage to pole a boat without tumbling myself into the water?" he filled in when she began floundering for words.

"No, I believe I am more astonished that you would wish to do so."

One of Everard's dark eyebrows shot upward in lofty fashion. "My dear Miss Sinclair, occasionally even *I* take pleasure in some of your rustic amusements."

Aurelia's heart sank. So he meant to play the dandy today, when she so longed for but one glimpse of his warm, encouraging smile. She watched unhappily as he rolled down his sleeves, rebuttoned his shirt with deliberate finesse, then shrugged his broad shoulders into his frock coat.

"I must apologize for my appearance," he drawled. "I, too, am finding this meeting most surprising. One does not expect to find a *lady* of such elegance sauntering through this wilderness." He cast a disparaging glance at her floppy-brimmed bonnet and the hem of her gray dress, steeped an inch in mud.

Aurechlia hugged her cloak more tightly around her.

"Oh, dear, Mr. Ramsey, you have caught me sadly out of fashion. I forgot 'tis all the crack now to wear one's silks and diamonds while trudging knee deep through the mire on one's estate."

"That does not appear to be all you've forgotten." Before she could guess his intent, Everard caught her wrist and wrestled her hand away from her pocket. In the next instant, he had pulled forth the gingerbread.

Aurelia suppressed a groan. She might have known those keen eyes of his would miss nothing. "Oh, that." She cringed under his accusing stare. "Mrs. McGinty gave it to me. I—I was taking it home to Effie."

"Indeed?" Everard whipped out his quizzing glass. Did the man never go anywhere without the damn thing? He proceeded to inspect the gingerbread man with mock solemnity. "Why, the unfortunate chap seems to have lost one of his feet. You don't by any chance have a mouse in your pocket, do you, Miss Sinclair?"

Aurelia bit her lower lip and glared at him, feeling very much like a little girl caught filching biscuits from the pantry. "No," she said chokingly. "If I had, I would have trained it straightaway to bite you."

She attempted to snatch the gingerbread from his hand, but he flung it far out into the broad, where it disappeared beneath the rippling waters with a soft plop. When his gaze shifted back to her, an angry spark flickered in his eyes.

"What the deuce did you think you were doing with that?"

"Well, to the best of my memory, I believe the pastime is called *eating*."

"Damn it, Aurelia. There is less than a fortnight before you leave for London."

"I am as perfectly capable of reading a calendar as you are, sir," she snapped. "And equally as aware that it matters naught how much time is left."

"Not if you intend to get up to such tricks as this the moment my back is turned."

"I would scarce describe this past month as *a moment*." Aurelia could have bitten out her tongue as soon as the words were out. She had no desire to give Ramsey the impression that she might have missed his daily visits. Aware that he was studying her with frowning surprise, she turned aside. "You may as well concede defeat, Mr. Ramsey. It is perfectly obvious you have given up the ridiculous task you set yourself—"

He caught her by the shoulders, spinning her around. "Whenever I cry quits, Miss Sinclair, you will be the first to know. And I will admit that, right now, the temptation is mighty strong." Despite his chiding words, a note of tender exasperation crept into his voice. "Stand still," he commanded when she attempted to wriggle away from him. Carefully he swept back the auburn curls, which the wind had tumbled about her cheeks, his fingers tangling in the fine strands. Then he forcefully straightened her ancient bonnet, retying the satin ribbon strings with a firm tug.

"There. That's better, but not much. Why are you not wearing any of your new things from London?"

Color spilled into Aurelia's cheeks, not entirely caused by the briskness of the weather. "None of those lovely gowns were meant for me. I feel like the vain crow in Aesop's fable, trying to borrow the peacock's feathers."

"The only time you look in the least like a crow, my dear, is when you run around garbed in these old rags. The next time I set eyes on you, you'd best be properly attired, or I swear I'll dress you myself."

He took much of the sting out of the threat by lightly chucking her under the chin. "And now," he said softly, "whatever put the idea into your head I had given up on you?"

Aurelia swallowed, suddenly feeling very foolish.

"You—you have grown so excessively critical of late. And I have had the feeling you are trying to avoid me."

"Despite what a frippery sort of fellow you think I am, Aurelia, I do have to attend to business occasionally."

She glanced toward the punt. "Indeed, 'tis remarkable how many gentlemen have pressing business upon the broads at the first hint of spring."

She meant the remark to be light, teasing, and was appalled to hear how shrewish she sounded. Justin had been gone months, and she had never penned him so much as one word of reproach. Why, then, was she waxing so peevish with Everard, upon whom she had no claim other than friendship? His next words made her feel even more ashamed of her behavior.

"I frequently pole down the stream from Aunt Lydia's, then out here amongst the shallows on the lake, when I want to be alone, when I need time to think through some difficulties."

"Difficulties?" For the first time, Aurelia noted the lines of weariness etched at the corners of his eyes. "I—I had no idea, Everard." Shyly, she squeezed his hand. "Why don't you tell me about them? Mayhap I could help."

Slowly Everard withdrew his fingers from her grasp. "I think not, my dear."

"That hardly seems fair. You know all of my deepest, darkest secrets."

But Everard merely shook his head, ignoring the coaxing note she infused into her voice. He retreated toward the bank, poking the toe of his boot at the green-tipped reeds. "A pity 'twere not later in the spring. I would have picked you some water lilies."

"I detest them. They smell like brandy." Aurelia trailed after him, determined not to let him change the subject. "Is it something to do with *The Albatross*?"

Everard's brow darkened into a frown. "How did you know about that?"

"Lady Foxcliff happened just to mention it one day."

Everard compressed his lips, although he said with forced lightness, "How very disconcerting. I thought the members of my family had all agreed to keep my bouts of insanity a secret."

"Your aunt was not being in the least critical," Aurelia hastened to add. "She has the deepest admiration for what she called a most daring and shrewd investment."

"Well, it seems my most daring and shrewd investment is now bits of flotsam off the coast of Brazil. A letter arrived from my solicitor a few days ago."

"Oh, Everard, I—I'm most dreadfully sorry." To Aurelia, her words seemed dreadfully inadequate. She reached out one hand to touch his sleeve, then allowed her arm to fall helplessly back to her side.

Everard stared out across the lake, his changeable blue eyes shifting with all the turbulence of the choppy waters. "Pure folly," he murmured as if he'd almost forgotten she was there. "Just as my father always said. But then, I've always been something of a fool about ships." She followed his gaze to where the silhouette of a sail scudded around a tree-lined bend out of view. "I was wont to dream of going to sea when I was a lad. Planned to follow in the footsteps of Lord Nelson."

He gave a soft, self-deriding laugh before wrenching his eyes back to Aurelia. "Could you picture it, Miss Sinclair? Me, a sailor?"

"Yes, I could," she said stoutly. Indeed, she suddenly had no difficulty imagining Everard upon the deck of a ship, clad only in dark, tight breeches outlining his powerful thighs, and a lace-cuffed white shirt, repelling hordes of Frenchmen swarming over the sides. Only not with a pistol; Everard would wield a sword.

"You are possessed of far too lively an imagination, Aurelia." She started, hearing a ripple of amusement in

Everard's voice, and was once again beset by the eerie feeling that he could read her thoughts.

He continued, "I fear the only deck I will ever command is that of cards, and none too successfully at that."

"Stuff! You only feel that way because your father is forever going on about Arthur—" She broke off at the shuttered look that came into Everard's eyes, warning her she was treading on forbidden ground.

"Aunt Lydia talks a great deal too much. I would never have guessed the pair of you had turned into such gossips."

Aurelia sensed she should let the subject drop, but found she could not. Her words tumbled out in a rush. "Your aunt only spoke of it because she worries about you, the quarrel with your father. I can well understand how you must have disliked your brother—"

"Not at all. I was very fond of Arthur until he was so inconsiderate as to die, leaving me to fill his shoes."

Aurelia summoned up all her courage to make her next suggestion. "Wouldn't it solve all your difficulties if—if you simply went home, made up the quarrel. Imagine what you must mean to your mother and father. Their only living son, their heir—"

Everard's harsh laugh halted her attempt at gentle persuasion. "How much I mean to them? My dear Miss Sinclair, do you know what happened the day after my brother was buried? A neighboring lord dropped by to pay his condolences." A bitter smile touched Everard's lips. "The poor fool thought to comfort my parents by pointing out to them that at least they were fortunate in having one son left to carry on the family name.

"My mother and father both looked at me. I think it was the first time it occured to either of them that I was now the sole surviving son. My mother burst into tears, and my father poured himself out a very large bumper of whiskey."

Aurelia felt a lump form in her throat. Despite his sardonic smile, she could see a vulnerability in his eyes that she knew all too well, having experienced it herself so often. From out across the lake came the harsh call of a teal, the melancholy sound piercing Aurelia with an aching sense of loneliness, the same loneliness she perceived in the towering man before her. She was beset by an overpowering longing to . . . She retreated a step, feeling confused, not quite knowing what it was she longed for. Unbidden tears welled in her eyes, one trickling down her cheek.

"That tale was meant to amuse you, Aurelia," Everard said, halting the course of the tear with a gentle stroke of his fingertip. "Not to make you look so glum. Don't waste your pity upon me, my dear. I am every bit as worthless as my father ever imagined."

Aurelia swallowed, then whispered vehemently, "No! I believe you could do anything in the world you put your mind to."

The rigid line of his mouth thawed into a half-doubting, half-grateful smile. "Thank you," he said. "If I am ever seeking a situation, I shall certainly apply to you for letters of character. I thought I might make a profession of bedeviling unfortunate young women with a penchant for gingerbread."

Aurelia emitted a watery chuckle. "I could certainly recommend you most heartily for that," she sniffed. "Indeed, if I did not know you were going to be there to bedevil me in London, I think I could scarce face the prospect of making such an exhibition of myself."

A startled expression crossed Everard's handsome features. He looked momentarily at a loss, then said haltingly. "Aurelia, I very much fear you are harboring a false impression. I will not be going to London."

"W-what?" Desperately, she scanned his solemn face, hoping for some twitch of the lips, some twinkle in the eye to indicate he was teasing her. The realization swept over her how much she had come to depend upon Everard. "Oh, n-no. But I thought you said you hadn't given up on me. You wouldn't be so cruel as to abandon me, would you?" She tried to make it sound like a jest, but her voice wavered and her fingers moved of their own volition to clutch at his sleeve.

He covered her hand with his own. "Aurelia, you won't need me. Justin will come to fetch you."

"No, he wrote to say he cannot come. He will meet me in London."

She winced at the sound of some words Everard muttered under his breath, although she only managed to distinguish the half of them that concerned Justin's parentage.

Almost as a form of habit, she rose to her betrothed's defense. "Well, he is extremely busy now that Parliament is in session."

"Parliament. If Justin ever saw the inside of the House of Lords, 'twas because—" Everard broke off in midsentence, looking extremely uncomfortable. "Ah, yes. That's true. I had forgotten Justin's strong interest in—in politics."

The statement was so ridiculous that when they eyed each other, neither could refrain from bursting into laughter. Aurelia was the first to recover, wiping her moist eyes and giving a little shrug.

" 'Tis quite beastly of you to oblige me to admit such things about Justin, but I know perfectly well he is off enjoying himself and has scarce given me a thought all winter. But you promised me you would change all that. How am I to go London without you? I shall make the most dreadful fool of myself at all the ton gatherings, and Justin will be ashamed of me."

"You will have Justin's mama to help you."

" 'Tis too close to the time of Clarice's confinement. I am to travel with Lady Foxcliff and stay at her town house

81

until the wedding. Effie will not even be accompanying me. The London air gives her headaches.''

"Well, Aunt Lydia may seem a bit rough in spots, and I fear she will be most lax as a chaperon, but you are a sensible woman and—and she does know her way around London society.''

"I need you," Aurelia persisted, her voice catching.

His eyes widened in shock.

"I—I am sorry," she faltered. "I should not have—"

"No, don't apologize," he murmured. " 'Tis just that . . . I believe that is the first time anyone has ever said that to me.'' She watched his eyes darken, the blue depths clouding as though some mighty conflict raged inside his mind, a conflict that seemed resolved when he raised his head to study her face.

That peculiar half smile crossed his lips again. "Your every wish is my command, my lady. If you truly *need* me when you journey up to London, I'll be there.''

"Everard!" she cried, joy and relief mingling in her voice. On a sudden impulse, she flung her arms about his neck and planted a swift kiss upon his cheek. Then she stepped back, appalled by her own boldness, yet not quite sorry, either.

"Goodness, 'tis so late," she said breathlessly. "I'd best get home before Effie thinks I have fallen in the lake and drowned.''

Barely giving him time to bid her farewell, Aurelia turned and struck out on the path for home. Everard stared after her until the last glimpse of auburn curls wisping from beneath that absurd bonnet vanished from sight. Then he stumbled toward the punt with movements entirely lacking in his usual grace.

The very devil! What had he done, promising her he would go to London? His fingers fumbled inside his waistcoat pocket, drawing forth the crumpled letter he had carried with him for days.

Albatross *last sighted going down in bad storm. . . . News has had bad effect upon your credit . . . Writs being sworn out for your arrest. . . . Strongly advise you stay out of London.*

The neat black scrawl blurred before Everard's eyes, the lines paling beside the memory of Aurelia's fiercely uttered words: *"I need you."*

Slowly he tore the letter to bits, casting the pieces adrift along the silver-gray waters of the lake. Nay, he was pledged to the task of helping this reluctant butterfly emerge from her chrysalis. No matter what perils lay ahead, 'twas too late to turn back now.

Everard touched his hand gingerly to his face, still feeling the petal-soft whisper of her mouth against his skin, as though the sensation were branded there. Aye. He grimaced. Far too late.

Chapter 6

Everard paced the length of the small front parlor in his aunt's fashionable London town house, which she had inherited from one of her numerous husbands. Hanging candle lanterns illuminated the parlor's walls of India Japan boards, the lower panels of which were carved with gilt flowers. 'Twas her ladyship's private jest to call the chamber her Smoking Room, for no matter how oft the chimney was cleaned, the flue still never seemed to draw properly.

Everard, however, was in no humor for jests of any kind. He strode to the parlor door, peered out at the circular marble stair curving up to the second floor, impatiently straightened the sleeves of his black superfine tailcoat, then resumed his pacing before the hearth.

"Why the devil isn't Justin here?" he growled. "After abandoning Aurelia all winter, the least he could do is arrive in time to escort her on her first evening in town."

"Pah! Aurelia isn't ready herself yet," Lady Foxcliff said. She shifted slightly on her Indian fan-stick chair, then rearranged her stiff mauve skirts over the painted satin cushion. With the heavy diamond necklet glittering about her throat and matching aigrette in her iron-gray hair, she resembled a mighty empress about to hold court, even more so when she glared at Everard with a most royal displeasure.

"Blast it all, Nevvy. Will you sit down before you wear a hole in that carpet? My first husband, Sir Thomas, imported it all the way from China, long before the Prince Regent stirred up the craze for Oriental foofaraw. Can't say it was ever to my taste, but always ahead of the times, my Thomas was."

Everard compressed his lips. In his present humor, he was ready to consign both the late Sir Thomas and his Oriental rug to perdition. His hand crept toward his cravat, and he nearly caught himself running a finger inside his neckcloth, an awkward gesture he never permitted himself to indulge in. He swore, locking his hands behind his back.

Damn folly this! He had told himself that with every turn of the hackney coach's wheels conveying him from his London lodgings to his aunt's town house. He had half expected a sinister shadow to come melting out of each corner, the burly arm of a tipstaff to stretch forth, dragging him off to debtors' prison. He must be mad thus to risk disgrace and ruin before he had opportunity to recoup his losses from *The Albatross*.

Aye, stark, raving mad. And his madness bore the form of misty green eyes alight with a simple faith that took his breath away. Aurelia. How she trusted, depended, upon him. He could not disappoint her, not even if it meant balancing upon the precipice of hell itself.

That, he assured himself was the only reason he had taken this great risk by coming to London. But even as the thought filtered through his mind, he knew himself for a liar. He had risked his freedom simply because he could not seem to stay away from the woman. The realization that he had fought to suppress all winter refused to be denied any longer. He had developed a strong attraction for the betrothed of his closest friend. How was he even going to look Justin squarely in the eye when he did arrive?

Everard slammed his fist down against the mahogany mantel, his mind filling with self-loathing. Blast it. He had known from the day he had taught her to waltz, felt her brushing against him, so warm, vibrant, that he was courting disaster. And she, in her innocence, had not the least notion what she was doing to him. He should have had the wit to refuse her entreaty to come to London. The temptation increased tenfold each time he was near her. Damn it all, Justin was the rakehell, not he. How could he betray his friendship with both Justin and Aurelia by allowing these unaccountable physical impulses to get the better of him?

"Go back to pacing again." Lady Foxcliff's barked command broke in upon his grim thoughts. "Better for you to wear out the carpets than to be thunking my poor old chimneypiece and pulling all those ferocious faces, as if you'd gone queer in the attic."

Everard spun on his heel to take another look out the study door. He wished Justin would arrive so that he could get this over with. Place Aurelia in Lord Spencer's care, watch her glide off in his arms, thus sweeping all temptation from Everard's path. Then he could return to his normal round of amusements, spending late evenings over the cards at White's. Perhaps he would even take a brief sojourn on the continent, he told himself, steadfastly ignoring the hollow feeling that accompanied the thought.

"Damnation," he said irritably. "Where is Aurelia? How can it possibly take you women so long to dress?"

"Humph! You're a fine one to talk. Now, dash it all, sit down before you drive me completely mad."

Before Everard could protest, Lady Foxcliff had seized him by the arm and tumbled him backward into a straight-legged Oriental chair. She rang for a glass of brandy, which Everard impatiently tossed off, scarce tasting the golden liquid. The fiery spirits burned his throat, but that seemed as nothing to the other burning sensations which had troubled him of late, keeping him awake nights, thinking about Aurelia. He set down the glass and proceeded to drum his fingers against the dark lacquered wood of the chair's arm.

Lady Foxcliff said nothing for several moments, but eyed him in a shrewd manner, which added to his discomfort.

"If you have something to say, kindly do so and stop regarding me as if I'd suddenly misplaced my head."

"Your head or your heart?" her ladyship asked. Everard glared at her. What the devil did she mean by that? His aunt's generous mouth split into an infuriating grin.

"Deuced odd. You've become remarkably surly. One minute snarling like a dog who has lost its bone, the next, looking all calf-eyed. If I didn't know better, I'd swear you'd fallen in love."

"Well, you do know better," Everard said curtly. "If I appear to have anything on my mind of late, 'tis money difficulties, not women."

"Dibs still not in tune, eh? Well, you'll come about when I pay off the wager, for I'm ready to concede the bet now. The changes you've wrought in Aurelia! Never seen the like in all my days. Pity she insists upon wasting herself on that scamp, Justin. If she manages to hang on to her wit along with her newfound looks, what a devastating effect she'll have on you poor hapless males."

Everard grimaced. Devastated. Aye, 'twas a fitting description of his present state. Aloud he snapped, "There is no wager. I told you before that I'd called that off. I never had any intentions of taking your money."

Abruptly he stood up and began to pace again.

Lady Foxcliff heaved a gusty sigh. "I expect you might as well finish off my carpet. Reely's already had her whack at it earlier this afternoon."

"If Aurelia is nervous, she's got good reason," Everard

said. "You would think that Justin would have called upon her first thing she arrived in town instead of keeping her waiting until right before Lady Carlisle's ball. The devil only knows what sort of mischief Justin has been up to this past winter."

"Did I hear someone slandering my name?" A cheerful male voice spoke up from the doorway. Everard stopped his pacing long enough to confront Justin's broad grin. The butler belatedly announced Lord Spencer's presence as he strode into the room. He planted a hearty buss on Lady Foxcliff's cheek, then proceeded to all but wring off Everard's hand by way of greeting.

"Best watch what you say about me, old fellow. I might be obliged to call you out, and I have no desire to end up on the point of your sword. I know *you* would never chose pistols."

The smile which had been coaxed from Everard froze. If Justin only knew how close he came to having a true reason to call him out.

Justin's eyes widened. " 'Twas only a jest, Ev." He gave Everard a rough clap on the shoulder. "You look as grim as a pallbearer who has misplaced the coffin. Don't tell me you finally wagered your sense of humor and lost that, too."

"Perhaps not lost so much as mislaid," Everard murmured. "How have you been?"

"Oh, in rare form." Justin craned his neck, peering about the room. "So, where's Reely? Have you been taking good care of her?"

"Prodigious good care," Lady Foxcliff said in dry tones, stealing a sly glance at Everard. He was annoyed to feel himself redden, although much of his feelings of guilt began to dissipate at the casual way Justin inquired after his intended bride.

"If you are so concerned about Aurelia's well-being," he said, "I would have thought you might have made some effort to return to Aldgate. 'Tis exceedingly difficult to plan a wedding without the bridegroom.''

"Lord, you sound like my mother. There's no great rush. I might as well be—I mean Aurelia should be permitted to enjoy the season first, before becoming leg-shackled." Justin strolled toward the far end of the room. He drew back the delicate gauze curtains, feigning deep interest in the coaches rumbling through Grosvenor Square.

Everard compressed his lips. "My sister Phillipa informs me she has not even seen announcement of the engagement in the *Post*."

"Er, well, I have not exactly found time to arrange that. Been busy, you know. Parliamentary sessions. Farm issues regarding Norfolk."

"Since when has Sylvie Fitzhurst been interested in debating the price of wheat? I hope you—"

Everard broke off when Lady Foxcliff lifted one finger to her lips and shushed him. She smiled at a point beyond Everard. "Good evening, Reely. Glad you have come down before Ev paces his way through the floor. He's been taking on worse than my second husband, Harry, when he was waiting for his favorite brood mare to foal."

Aurelia's silvery laugh sounded in Everard's ear. Spinning around to look at her, 'twas all he could do not to catch his breath. She stood silhouetted in the doorway, her perfect oval-shaped face drained of all color except for one rosy spot glowing in each petal-smooth cheek. Her soft pink lips parted in an apprehensive smile as she nervously twisted that hideous, gaudy betrothal ring.

Slowly, Everard permitted his eyes to wander from the glossy auburn ringlets caressing the slender white column of her throat, his gaze traveling down to encompass full, round breasts and gently curving hips accented by a high-waisted gown of pearl-colored satin. Dainty kid slippers peeked out from under the hem, which was embroidered with garlands of gilt leaves and coral roses. Her trim waist was banded by a belt of narrow gold ribbon.

"Well, my dear, you'll turn quite a few heads tonight, I vow." Lady Foxcliff said. "You'll make all these London wenches look like a parcel of sway-backed mules. Stap me, Ev, you must take the money. Never was a wager so fairly won."

Everard shot his aunt a quelling frown, but Aurelia appeared not to have heeded her ladyship's remark. Her regard never wavered from Everard. He sensed that she was awaiting for some sign of his approval, but he found himself at a loss for words. She was beautiful, dazzlingly beautiful, more so than he had even dared imagine. But her radiance came not so much from the elegant clothes, the transformation in her figure, nor the new coiffure. The true source of enchantment lay in those expressive eyes of hers that had so captivated him from the very beginning. Tonight they shone like polished emeralds, the glittering facets reflecting all her hidden depths of passion, her fears, her longings, her dreams . . . the eyes of a woman about to fly to the arms of the man she loved.

Everard lowered his gaze as though shielding his sight from a too brilliant sun. From behind him, he heard Justin exclaim in jocular tones, "I say, Ramsey, you sly dog. You have been holding out on me."

Aurelia started, then blushed as if becoming aware of Lord Spencer's presence in the room for the first time. Everard noted how she tensed, her breathless expectation as Justin elbowed his way past Everard. His teeth flashed in his most engaging grin.

"I will contrive to forgive you, Ev, if you present me to this ravishing creature at once."

Everard folded his arms across his chest, supposing that, as always, Justin meant to pull off one of his cow-handed jests. But one look at the rapt expression on Justin's face told him otherwise. Good Lord, the man truly didn't recognize Aurelia.

Justin gave Everard a sharp, eager nudge, hissing under his breath. "What's the matter with you, Ev? Present me."

Everard rolled his eyes heavenward, then said in his driest tones, "Miss Sinclair, allow me to introduce you to a gentleman perishing to make your acquaintance, your fiancé, Lord Spencer."

"How do you do?" Aurelia sank into a curtsy. The moment was too solemn for her even to smile. Everard heard Justin suck in his breath with a great whoosh. He took two faltering steps forward, squinting at Aurelia like an ancient grandsire whose eyesight was failing him.

"R-reely?" All color drained from Justin's face. As he sank back, Lady Foxcliff shoved a chair under him.

"Ha!" She guffawed. "Ring for Jervis to bring the boy some smelling salts. Better yet, have a swig of this." She forced a huge swallow of brandy between Justin's lips, then whacked him vigorously on the back when he began to choke.

"Been waiting years to give you a start like this, you young rapscallion. Did you think I'd ever forgot the time you dressed up that sheep in my best nightgown and stuck it in my bed?"

And Lady Foxcliff went off into peals of mirth at Justin's befuddled expression. Everard glowered at the two of them in mounting irritation, before making his way to Aurelia's side. Her smile seemed plastered on her face. Everard didn't know exactly what Aurelia had been expecting from this moment, but he was certain it was not this farce. He started to place his arm about her stiff shoulders, then stopped himself.

"Blast it all, Justin," he said. "She hasn't changed that much, if you'd only had the wit to use your eyes before."

Aurelia's lips trembled, but she managed to reply, "I

91

daresay the problem was Justin never had a quizzing glass."

"Quizzing glass. I'm beginning to think I must need spectacles." Justin staggered to his feet. He peered at Aurelia once more. "I must be dreaming. Someone slap me awake."

"I would be only too happy to oblige," Everard said between gritted teeth.

"This is utterly incredible! Who in his wildest imagination would ever have thought that—ow." Justin broke off when the toe of Everard's boot crushed down upon his foot. For once Everard's dark looks of warning penetrated through even Lord Spencer's thick sensibilities.

"Er, yes. Just so." Justin floundered, straightening his cravat until he appeared to have regained command of himself. "My dearest Reely . . . Aurelia," he quickly amended when Everard's boot found its mark again. "You look absolutely stunning. Can you blame me for being so overcome?"

He reached for Aurelia's hand, raising it to his lips with a practised gesture, holding her gaze for just the right length of time, infusing his gray eyes with just the right amount of sincerity. "My beautiful fairy-tale princess, forgive me and say that you will favor your awkward cavalier with the first waltz this evening."

Aurelia's reply was all but inaudible, but she managed to nod. A tremor shot through her slender frame as she stared down at the carpet like a bashful country girl.

Damn it, Aurelia, Everard longed to scold her. You look like a queen. Raise your head and carry yourself regally. The woman still did not realize her own worth, that she was indeed conferring a great favor upon the graceless Justin.

Justin linked his arm through hers, and the two of them strolled from the room, heads bent together, whispering as though not another person existed in the world. Aurelia did not even so much as glance back at Everard.

Lady Foxcliff gave her nephew a sharp poke in the ribs. "Well, you've done it, my boy. Dished Justin something proper. Congratulations."

Everard made no response; his mouth had gone suddenly dry. He waited for the sense of triumph he had once expected to feel at this moment, but it was not forthcoming.

'Twas exactly as Aurelia had always dreamed. The ballroom spun out before her, a dizzying array of marble panels, mirrors, floral swags, and great fluted Corinthian pilasters. Crystal chandeliers blazed overhead but were no more glittering than the assembled company, the ladies resplendent in their colorful silk gowns, set off like bright jewels by the more somber black evening attire of the men.

Justin pressed close to her side, smiling down at her with a possessive pride. Exactly like her dream.

Then why did she feel this strong urge to tear herself from Justin's side and run to Everard, cling to his hand like a frightened child? She stole a glance over her shoulder to where he walked behind, escorting his aunt. His features were already schooled into an expression of bored indifference, but he relaxed long enough to give her an encouraging smile that seemed oddly tinged with melancholy.

Aurelia stiffened her spine, trying to concentrate as Justin presented her to their hostess, Lady Carlisle. The vivacious brunette subjected Aurelia to a critical inspection before beginning to fawn over Justin. Aurelia tried to appear at ease, fixing an unconcerned smile upon her face. If only she were not so miserably conscious of all the ladies' eyes trained in her direction, the whispers behind the painted fans. And the men were even worse, ogling her without even attempting to hide the fact. Why, one gaunt, pale fellow by the musicians' platform actually craned his neck.

Aurelia froze, feeling the blood drain from her face. No, it could not be. But there was no mistaking the colorless eyes, the skin stretched taut over angular bones, the thinning hair plastered to the small skull. Augustus Snape. As her gaze locked with his, she saw Snape's mouth go slack with startled recognition. Then he recovered, sweeping her an insolent bow. Although she might have forgotten his existence, she could tell from his smirk he had never forgotten her. Her mind drifted back to that dreadful day in the parlor when Snape had bruised her wrist, threatening her with his vengeance. She shivered.

"Aurelia? Is something wrong?" Everard's voice murmured close to her ear. "You look as though you had seen a corpse." He seemed to sense at once who had disconcerted her and leveled his quizzing glass at Snape's cadaverlike frame. "By God, you have!"

Snape appeared about to approach, but the stony expression on Everard's face apparently made him think better of it. The man melted back into the throng of other guests.

Everard gave a snort of disgust. "The Carlisles were never noted for being particular about whom they invite to these affairs." He glanced down at Aurelia, frowning. "I take it you are acquainted with that walking collection of ill-assorted bones?"

Aurelia nodded, moistening her lips. She suddenly felt very foolish. After all, she knew what a coward Snape was, and the notion that the man could still be harboring some sort of a grudge was pure melodrama. She forced herself to shrug and say, " 'Tis only someone who used to live at Aldgate. No one of any consequence."

She sensed that Everard did not believe her, but before he could pursue the matter further, the orchestra struck up the strains of a waltz. Aurelia's pulses quickened in time to the music. She remembered how it had felt gliding through the steps of the dance in Everard's arms. So warm, so exhilarating.

Justin stepped in front of Everard, giving Aurelia a heart-melting smile. "I believe this is our dance, my dear."

"Oh. Of course." Aurelia turned to excuse herself to Everard, but he was already gone. Her feet felt peculiarly leaden as Justin spun her out onto the dance floor, but she held her breath, waiting for the magic to overtake her. After all, this was Justin, the man she loved, holding her so close to his tall frame. But something was dreadfully wrong.

Justin's arm banded her far too tight. She had scarce room to breathe, let alone move. As she tried to concentrate on her steps, his lips brushed close to her ear. She prayed he was not going to call her "his beautiful fairy-tale princess" again. She had nearly dissolved into hysterical laughter the last time he had done so.

But she had longed all her life for Justin to murmur tender words to her. Aye, tender, she thought, but not ludicrous. Then she felt promptly ashamed of herself for being so critical and dissatisfied. When Justin guided her the length of the ballroom, she stumbled over his feet.

After that first misstep, she seemed incapable of regaining her balance, all that Everard had taught her fleeing her mind. When Justin tugged one way, Aurelia found herself dipping in the opposite direction. Her cheeks burned, certain that everyone present was remarking how clumsy she was. 'Twas exactly like the assemblies in Aldgate, only worse. At home she had not been such an object of curiosity. What was wrong with her? She had danced so beautifully with Everard that day.

Mayhap you simply never had the right partner.

The memory of Everard's words echoing through her head startled her. Justin gasped when she trod down hard upon his instep.

"Ow," he yelped, his newfound gallantry momentarily forgotten. "Hang it all, Reely, between you and Everard, I shall end up lame."

Before Aurelia could ask what Justin meant by his odd reference to Everard, he whirled her around, blundering into another couple. Aurelia stepped on a gold-spangled train.

"I beg your pardon."

"You—you stupid, clumsy . . ." The woman's voice trailed off into incoherent rage that seemed far out of proportion to what had occurred. Adjusting the décolletage of her exceedingly low-cut gown, the blond-haired woman thrust out a pouting red lip. Eyes like pale blue ice chips glared at Aurelia as if . . .

As if she hated me, Aurelia thought in bewilderment. Merely for stepping on her gown?

"Beg pardon, Sylvie," Justin muttered. "Er, I mean, Lady Silvie."

The woman favored him with a killing glance before she swept her skirts aside, then stalked off the dance floor, leaving her astonished partner to hasten after her. Aurelia started to ask Justin who the extremely choleric lady was, but he twirled her in an awkward circle, hastily beginning to pay compliments about Aurelia's eyes, comparing them to sapphires. He waxed so poetic Aurelia did not have the heart to remind him her eyes were green.

From the shadow of one of the pilasters, Lady Sylvie Fitzhurst glared at the couple. "Clumsy cow!"

Augustus Snape observed the blond beauty's rage with sneering amusement. Smoothing down the straggling wisps of his hair, he wended his way to Lady Silvie's side.

"Good evening, milady. What! All alone?"

Lady Sylvie eyed Snape with intense dislike. "No. Unfortunately, you're here."

Unperturbed, Snape flicked open an enamel snuffbox, raising a pinch to his thin nostrils. "Ah, I beg your pardon for disturbing you when you are so preoccupied. I see you are extremely taken with Lord Spencer's intended bride.''

''That cloddish stick of a female?'' Sylvie tossed her head. ''So very thin. She looks as though she were dying of consumption.''

''But surely you must find her presence in London highly diverting. Or could it be that you had begun to nourish hopes that Lord Spencer would never bring her from Aldgate, that mayhap he had forgotten all about her?''

Beneath the layers of pearl powder and rouge, Lady Sylvie Fitzhurst's cheeks were mottled an unbecoming shade of red. She was not about to admit the fact to a disgusting creature like Snape, but that was exactly what she had begun to hope. The engagement had not even been formally announced in the papers. Aurelia Sinclair's presence at the Carlisle ball had come as a nasty shock, the more so because Sylvie had formed a far different impression of Lord Spencer's betrothed. She had imagined some dowdy country wench whom his lordship was being pressured to marry out of a sense of duty. And men had been led astray from their duty before.

Why, only last autumn Sir Barton Crumm had eloped with his mistress, and now his family found themselves forced to acknowledge her. Sylvie had laid her own plans then, plans that the lovely Miss Sinclair seemed to have put to rout. Of course, she had several other prospects she kept dangling, in case of failure with Justin, but none of them were nearly as attractive as the possibility of becoming a marchioness.

Snape chuckled softly. ''So depressing, is it not, my dear? After you invested so much time in Lord Spencer, were so generous with your attentions.''

Sylvie's fingers curled until her nails bit into her palms. ''Why don't you seek out some company more congenial with your station, Mr. Snape? I am sure you can find any number of stable boys out in the yard.''

"Tch, tch, my dear. How unkind, when I only meant to sympathize. When Lord Spencer announced his engagement, my own hopes were quite cut up as well as yours."

Sylvie arched her brows, then emitted a shrill laugh. "You and Miss Sinclair? I find that extremely difficult to believe."

Snape's smiling lips hardened for a moment. He thrust out his thin chest. "Well, I *am* connected to the Marquess of Scallingsforth. And Miss Sinclair was not always the dazzling creature who is now inspiring you to such spasms of jealousy. Only last summer, she was a deal plumper and dressed more like a housekeeper than the mistress of a great estate."

Sylvie sniffed, staring at the whirling circle of dancers waltzing past her. She reflected that it would have been much easier to deal with a plump, plain rival than the auburn-haired sylph who was holding herself so woodenly in Justin's arms. "Then by what miracle was she transformed?"

The muscles of Snape's gaunt face tensed into an expression of brooding. "I don't know. But even miracles run a risk of being undone, my lady. And I have an account to settle with Miss Aurelia Sinclair." His features relaxed into their customary leer. "So you see, Lady Sylvie, you are not alone in your desire to rescue Lord Spencer from what could prove a most disastrous engagement."

For the first time since she had set eyes upon Aurelia Sinclair, Sylvie saw a glimmer of light amongst the dark ruin of her schemes. Her mouth widened into a feline smile. "My dear Mr. Snape," she said, taking his arm. "Do tell me more." They drifted off in the direction of a private alcove just as the waltz was coming to an end.

Strange, Aurelia reflected, when the last chords of music sounded in her ear. Once all she had longed for was to be taken into Justin's arms; now she moved out of them with a feeling of considerable relief. Everything was happening too quickly, she told herself. If only she had time to be alone with Justin, then all would be well. But she scarce had time to draw breath before she found herself surrounded by an army of broad male shoulders crowding forward, clamoring for the next quadrille. Yet the one perfectly starched white cravat she looked for was missing. No mocking blue eyes twinkled down to reassure her; no teasing, sensitive mouth quirked into a half smile. Everard appeared to have completely vanished. Had he already left the ball? The thought made her feel inexplicably weary, but she forced herself to smile at her next partner, a dashing young man whose high, starched shirt collars threatened to wreak havoc upon his earlobes.

Although Aurelia did not quite disgrace herself with Mr. Comstock as she had with Justin, she moved through the dance with more precision than enthusiasm. Were all London men so entirely wanting in conversation?

"I vow, Miss Sinclair," her partner lisped. "You take the shine out of all the other ladies. I can tell you will be the new ornament of the season."

"Ornament, sir? That sounds most alarming. Do you think people will wish to hang me?"

"I—I beg your pardon?" Mr. Comstock's large brown eyes went amazingly blank. Aurelia sighed. As she went down the rest of the dance she amused herself by imagining what retort Everard would have flung back at her.

So this was what it was like to be a much sought after belle, perpetually on display like a waxworks figure, prized only for the molding of one's figure, the elegant clothes bedecking one's back. Aurelia winced, feeling a blister begin to form on her heel. There was something to be said for spending the evening propped against the wall after all.

But, she reminded herself, she had not endured months of starvation to become a social success. She had done so with the idea of winning Justin's love. Firmly excusing herself to the portly baronet bearing down upon her to claim the next cotillion, Aurelia set off in search of her betrothed. She spotted him bending over Lady Carlisle, laughing far too loudly at something that coy beauty had said.

Frowning, Aurelia started in that direction only to be intercepted by a cool, slender hand laid upon her arm.

"Pray, Miss Sinclair, don't rush off," a feminine voice cooed. "Our acquaintance has gotten off to such a bad beginning."

Aurelia turned to confront the voluptuous blonde whose dress she had stepped upon during the waltz. What had Justin called her—Lady Sylvie? Her previous ill humor obviously forgotten, the woman was smiling at Aurelia in the sweetest manner imaginable.

"I am Lady Sylvie Fitzhurst, an old, old friend of Justin's."

"Indeed?" Aurelia asked politely, all the while wondering why this old, old friend of Justin's had only moments ago looked as if she would have liked to thrust a dagger through his heart.

As though she guessed what Aurelia was thinking, Lady Sylvie gave a tinkling laugh. "Pray excuse my earlier display of bad temper. Such a crush of people. It does so wear upon one's nerves. I would have left at once but, I have been longing to meet you. Justin has told me so much about you. I had no idea you had been so shockingly ill."

"Ill?" Aurelia blinked in astonishment. She could not recall ever having been sick a day in her life.

Lady Sylvie's soft voice oozed sympathy. "A wasting sickness of some kind, was it my dear?"

"N-no," Aurelia said, beginning to wish she had taken a little more time to study herself in the mirror before she had left her bedchamber. But she had been far too eager to hasten downstairs and gauge Everard's reaction.

Lady Sylvie linked her arm through Aurelia's, pulling

her along. "You look so fatigued and so pale. That Justin! Such a careless one. I'll wager he's been too busy flirting with Lady Carlisle and has not been looking after you."

'Twas perfectly true that Justin did seem to be paying an inordinate amount of attention to Lady Carlisle. And only moments ago he had whispered some nonsense in Aurelia's ear about being so dazzled by her brillance that he did not even see any of the lesser stars on the horizon. Aurelia supposed she should be feeling vexed, but her emotions seemed tangled into a hopeless ball of confusion.

"I know you provincials—" Lady Sylvie coughed, then amended, "I mean you ladies from the *country* are not accustomed to supping at such a late hour. You must be perishing for want of food."

As Lady Sylvie steered her in the direction of the dining room, Aurelia was about to protest that she was not in the least hungry, only quite fatigued. But her words faltered at the sight of bewigged footmen in scarlet livery scurrying to lay covers upon a long, narrow buffet table. In the center of the gold and marble chamber stood a table cleverly decorated to appear like a plantation of flowering shrubs. Two silver dolphins arose amidst the greenery, spouting streams of water into a crystal fountain. Clustered around the centerpiece were iced creams, cakes, sweetmeats, and every possible sort of confection Aurelia could have imagined.

She closed her eyes, feeling a surge of weakness coming over her. She had been especially good since that afternoon Everard had caught her with the gingerbread, determined not to disappoint him. But Everard wasn't here. He might have troubled himself to dance with me at least once, Aurelia thought with a sudden stab of resentment. And after he had promised faithfully to support her through this ordeal.

Her fingers closed reflexively over the china plate Sylvie Fitzhurst pressed into her hand. Aurelia stared down into a succulent heap of macaroons and small frosted cakes.

"A little sustenance will do you no end of good, my dear," Lady Sylvie purred. "Can't have you fainting before supper is served your first evening in town. You will need your strength. I am sure you have a long time to go until your wedding day."

Wedding day? The words jolted Aurelia. In the midst of all the preparations, the anticipation of seeing Justin again, she had nigh forgotten her main reason for coming to London, to be married. Nervously, she began to nibble on one of the macaroons.

It scarce surprised her when the plate was snatched from her hand. She had but to take a bite of something sweet for Everard Ramsey to rise up before her like some dark, avenging angel. But rather than feeling discomfited, she was flooded with a sensation akin to relief when his piercing blue eyes regarded her with stern reproof.

"I believe you have forgotten this is our dance, Miss Sinclair," he said in clipped tones.

Her mouth full of coconut, Aurelia could not reply. Sylvie insinuated herself between them. "Why, my dear Mr. Ramsey. I had no notion you were back in town."

She fluttered long, sultry lashes up at him, her eyes devouring his broad shoulders and lean hips with more appetite than Aurelia had for the macaroon that turned dry as dust in her mouth. She swallowed hard as Lady Sylvie dipped closer to Everard. His gaze flicked briefly down her plunging neckline. Aurelia nearly choked. Uncertain of her opinion of Lady Sylvie before, she took a violent dislike to the woman.

With a pretty pout, Sylvie extended one hand to Everard, clearly waiting for her fingertips to be kissed. "I am inclined to be angry with you, sir. Why ever have you not come to call upon me?"

"Alas," Everard drawled. "I expect it is because I have never liked crowds. There appears to be such a press of other gentlemen departing from your home at all hours."

As Lady Sylvie went rigid with shock, he slowly turned her outstretched hand palm upward and balanced the confiscated plate of desserts upon her hand. With another affable nod at the outraged lady, he seized Aurelia by the arm, dragging her out of the dining parlor.

Aurelia stole one glance over her shoulder at Lady Sylvie. The woman looked very much as though she wanted to fling the dish at Everard's retreating back. "Everard," Aurelia gasped on a half laugh. "That was abominably rude."

"All part of my image. 'Tis expected of me."

"Don't I know it!" Aurelia struggled to pull her arm free from his grasp, remembering that she should be annoyed with him. "I don't recall in the least having promised to dance with you, which is not surprising. I have scarce seen you all evening."

Everard halted under the archway leading into the ballroom. "And you, Miss Sinclair, know full well why I was forced to say that."

"Ah, yes. I was actually about to—heaven forbid—enjoy myself. Tell me, sir. Do you expect me to live on rice and vinegar for the rest of my life?"

"No, I merely expect you to behave sensibly. I didn't devote my entire winter preparing you for this night to have you waste it gorging yourself on sweets."

Aurelia's chin snapped up, her eyes locking with his own smoldering blue ones. "Mayhap what I chose to gorge upon is no longer your concern, sir. You never seem to trouble yourself unless—"

Aurelia broke off, her face flushing as she became aware their quarrel was attracting no little attention. Behind her, an elderly gentleman coughed, waiting to escort a portly dame into the ballroom. Aurelia and Everard squarely blocked the entryway. Everard noticed this embarrassing circumstance at the same moment as she did. Fixing a look of rigid politeness upon his face, he linked his arm through Aurelia's, propelling her forward.

The musicians struck up the notes of another waltz. The melody drifted hauntingly to Aurelia's ears. 'Twas the same waltz Effie had thunked out on the pianoforte that long-ago day. How uncomplicated her life had seemed then. Aurelia sighed deeply, feeling her anger dissolve.

Impulsively she tugged at Everard's sleeve. "Everard." She refused to be daunted by the icy glint when he regarded her. "I—I am sorry for being such a shrew. I believe this is your dance, after all. Do come and waltz with me."

His long, dark lashes lowered, concealing the expression in his eyes. "No."

"Why not?"

" 'Twould utterly ruin my reputation," he explained in self-mocking tones. "Dandies, my dear Aurelia, do not dance attendance upon young ladies at these affairs. Rather they find a convenient pillar to lean upon, cross their arms, and look insufferably bored."

So saying, he located one of the carved pilasters and proceeded to demonstrate. Aurelia smiled coaxingly. "Can you not make an exception this once?"

"I am afraid not. You have no need of me. 'Tis not as though you were suffering from a dearth of partners."

"No, I suppose I cannot complain of that," Aurelia said slowly, although she felt if she were obliged to listen to another set of lavish compliments, she was going to scream. Every man in the room tonight, including Justin, had told her how dazzling she looked, every man that is except for the one whose opinion she valued the most. Everard had not said one word about her appearance. Was he disappointed in her? Had she failed to meet his exacting expectations?

"Aurelia," he cut into her thoughts. " 'Tis going to be

exceedingly difficult for me to keep staring disdainfully at this rabble if you are going to stand in front of me looking so forlorn. Now, what is amiss?'' His voice suddenly sharpened. "Has Justin been saying or doing anything he oughtn't?''

"Oh, no. In fact, he has been making me all manner of pretty speeches. 'Tis just . . .'' She hesitated, biting her lip. Her fingers fidgeted with the neckline of her gown. "You have never said if—if my appearance meets with your approval.''

Everard's brow furrowed, his hand moving instinctively toward his quizzing glass. Aurelia gripped his wrist, halting the movement, forcing him to meet her gaze.

After a lengthy pause, he said, "You look—presentable.''

The cold words would have stung Aurelia if his eyes had not told her otherwise. He tried to stare at a point past her, but as though he could not help it, his gaze traced every line of her face, lingering on the silhouette of her curves with an appreciation that appeared increasingly warmer, until Aurelia suddenly felt as though she were glowing. Her hand slipped down his wrist to be crushed within the pressure of his strong fingers.

"I have never yet thanked you,'' she said softly, "for all you've done for me, for giving me—''

"I've done nothing,'' he said abruptly, his voice going hoarse. "There is not one thing I gave you that you did not always possess.''

A blush heated her cheeks, which none of the flattery she had received all evening had been able to produce.

"So what mischief have the two of you been about?'' Aurelia felt Justin's arm encircle her waist almost at the same moment Everard dropped her hand as though it were a live coal.

"What the deuce do you mean by that?'' Everard snapped.

Justin gaped from her to Everard and then back again. "Why, nothing in particular. Only that the pair of you looked so remarkably serious when I walked up just now, I—." Justin frowned. "I declare neither of you seem able to appreciate a jest anymore."

Everard's face was oddly tinted with red, but he resumed his position by the pillar, saying in his customary languid manner, "You know I never find anything in the least diverting about these tedious affairs, Justin. Why don't you attempt to amuse Miss Sinclair? I have the distinct impression she would like to dance."

"An excellent suggestion. Reely?" Justin gave her a melting smile. Aurelia permitted him to lead her away, but her heart misgave her. The last thing she desired was another awkward session on the dance floor with Justin. She glanced wistfully back at Everard, who was already engaged in conversation with Mr. Comstock. The gentleman preened, showing off the lapels of his new jacket. Aurelia was not close enough to hear Everard's remark, but from the quirk of his mouth, 'twas obviously something cutting. The young man's puffed out chest deflated.

Justin tugged at Aurelia's hand to regain her attention, but she stepped out of the circle of his embrace. "Please," she protested. "I am so hot. Mayhap we could sit down for a moment."

Justin's eyes gleamed in a manner Aurelia found disconcerting. "Oh, I think we can do better than that," he said. He led her to a small curtained alcove behind one of the ballroom's Grecian sculptures, a statue of Venus. A long French window stood ajar, letting in wisps of cool air that Aurelia found refreshing until she realized how close Justin stood next to her.

They were now quite alone. But this was the very thing she had always wished for, wasn't it? He turned her slowly to face him.

"I thought I would never wrest you away from all your

other admirers. I have been waiting for this all evening," he said huskily.

"Truly?" she asked, swallowing the urge to comment that it had been excessively kind of Lady Carlisle to entertain Justin while he waited. But it seemed a remark likely to destroy the romance of the moment. She was secluded with a most handsome man, the man she loved, she reminded herself. Beyond the dark panes of glass, a silver crescent of moon skated across the night sky. And she was about to receive her first kiss.

Aurelia stared as Justin's bronzed features bent closer, waiting for the wild thumping of her heart, the racing of her pulses she'd always expected.

His lips a breath away, Justin paused. "Umm, Aurelia, 'twould help considerably if you would close your eyes."

"Oh. Sorry," she mumbled, promptly complying with his suggestion. She felt the warmth of his lips press against her own. The sensation was interesting, she decided, and not altogether unpleasant.

Justin drew back, and Aurelia risked a glance at him. His brow was puckered with anxious concern and a shadow of chagrin. Aurelia felt she ought to apologize, but she was not quite sure for what. 'Twas unfortunate the moment she had longed for most of her life should occur when she felt so utterly drained by the confusing emotions she'd experienced this evening.

She wrapped her arms around Justin's neck, trying to spark more enthusiasm into their next kiss. His lips crushed down harder, more demanding this time. The physical aspects of love must be greatly overrated, Aurelia decided sadly. All kissing did was make one's front teeth ache. Something to be endured, just as her mother had always told her. She had so hoped that for once her mother would be proven wrong.

As she searched her mind for some polite way to indicate to Justin she felt suffocated, the sound of a muttered oath grated upon her ears. Aurelia wrenched her head away from Justin's lips and twisted toward the alcove's entrance. Everard stood, one hand frozen upon the curtain, his features pulled taut into a expression of stone. He might have been a statue except for the storm-shadowed depths of his eyes.

Aurelia yanked free of Justin's arms, pressing her hands to her heated cheeks. The agonizing moment seemed to drag out forever until Everard's mask of impassivity settled back into place. Addressing himself to Justin, he said, "I am sorry. It appears we both had the same idea. I mean," he added hastily, "about getting a breath of air."

Justin gave him a lazy grin. "Quite all right, old fellow. Don't distress yourself over it."

Everard nodded curtly. Spinning on his heel, he strode out of the alcove without saying a word to her. Aurelia's spirits plummeted. Had she shocked Everard with her behavior? Surely 'twas no sin to kiss one's own fiancé. Why, then, did she feel she had done something terribly wrong?

Justin began to draw Aurelia back into his arms. "Now what were we about? Oh, yes . . ." But as his lips drew near hers again, Aurelia quickly buried her face in his jacket. She closed her eyes, the image of Everard's tense features seeming branded upon the lids. "Justin," she said in muffled accents, "C-could you please take me back to Lady Foxcliff's? I—I have the most splitting headache."

Just beyond the curtain, Everard caught one last glimpse of Aurelia nestling herself against Justin's shoulder, molding to his friend's tall frame as though she had always belonged there. Everard spun on his heel and strode across the ballroom, seeking out the one room he'd avoided all night.

Inside the spacious drawing room, groups of men gathered about the small green baize card tables. When Lord

Carlisle beckoned him to join them, Everard compressed his lips, taking a seat. But for the first time in his life, when he cut a deck of cards, his fingers trembled. He scarce saw the black spades, the hearts, or diamonds staring up at him, did not know whether he held aces or deuces. All he saw was Aurelia locked in Justin's arms, fervently returning his embrace. He relived the moment over and over again, the memory piercing him with sword-point swiftness. As the queen of hearts fumbled from his hand, landing face up before his opponents, he realized the true nature of his folly regarding Aurelia. Not friendship. Not physical attraction. Damn it all to hell, he was in love with the woman.

Chapter 7

Aurelia awoke to the sound of iron wheels and horses' hooves ringing on the cobblestone pavement beneath her bedchamber window. She groaned, stuffing her head under the feather-tic pillow. During the fortnight she had been in London, she had yet to accustom herself to the perpetual bustle of the streets. Nor to the infernal sounds of the charleys making their rounds all night long, singing out, "Three o'clock and all-ll is wee-eell."

But all was not well, Aurelia thought irritably. Her head throbbed, and her mouth was stuffed with cotton waddings. She touched a finger experimentally to her lips. No, 'twas not cotton. 'Twas her tongue. Flinging the pillow aside, she rolled over with another small moan. Bright sunlight streamed past the silk hangings, telling her that the hour was well advanced. She forced her stiff, aching muscles out of bed, surveying the room with bleary eyes. The airy, well-appointed chamber was decorated with a parchment-colored wallpaper, hand painted in a delicate design of young trees, with tiny birds nesting here and there in the fragile branches. But the bucolic scene did little to soothe the pounding behind her temples.

She rang for her maid, then shrugged painfully into a linen wrapper, easing her feet into a pair of velvet mules. Padding across the carpeted floor, she squinted into a bamboo-framed mirror. Dark-ringed eyes that seemed over-large in her pale face peered back at her; her auburn curls drooped dejectedly about her shoulders. So this was what one looked like the morning after a night spent in dissipated merriment, sipping too much champagne in an effort to appear gay and carefree. She could have passed for an orphaned waif or—or a woman completely down on her luck, who had lost her last friend.

If not her last friend, then certainly her dearest. Aurelia glanced toward a small cabriole-legged vanity, where her tortoiseshell brushes were all but buried beneath an avalanche of invitations and calling cards. Not one of the elegant gilt-edged rectangles of vellum had come from Everard Ramsey.

Aurelia bit down on her lip to keep it from trembling. At least, she had once thought Everard was her friend. But friends did not desert one simply because—because . . . Aurelia could not think of a single reason why Everard should do so. Had it anything to do with his strange reaction to her kissing Justin at the ball? Everard might be something of a stickler about the proprieties, but he was not that old-fashioned in his notions, nor in the least a prude.

More likely that now he was no longer *buried in the wilds of Norfolk*, as he put it, he could return to his former amusements amongst the dandy set. Doubtlessly, he presumed all her time to be taken up with Justin. Which, of course, was exactly how it should be, Aurelia reminded herself, wincing at the red glare of her engagement ring.

The door to the bedchamber slammed open. Aurelia grimaced, feeling the loud sound reverberate, sending waves of pain to the very roots of her hair.

"Wallis," she hissed at her maid.

"Beg pardon, Miss Aurelia." The apple-cheeked young woman closed the door with another excrutiating thud. "Oh, miss," she exclaimed, the ribbons on her mob cap flying, "I was just making haste to wake you. Lord Spencer is already below stairs waiting."

Aurelia stared at the girl in surly silence. What of it, she wanted to ask, entirely forgetting, in her present misery, that at one time she would have sold the hair off her head to receive such tidings.

Wallis's cheery manner withered under Aurelia's glare. "Will—will miss be wanting her glass of vinegar this morning?"

"No!" Aurelia said emphatically. Her stomach turned over at the very thought.

While Wallis filled the wash basin and tiptoed about to lay out her clothes, Aurelia undressed herself with deliberate slowness. She had no cause to complain of Lord Spencer's inattentiveness these days, she told herself morosely. He was forever at her side, escorting her to the routs, the theater, the park. Although his ardor was extremely gratifying, 'twould have been pleasant, just once, to enjoy a quiet cup of tea without feeling Justin's arm stealing about her waist. Couldn't he ever simply say that he loved her without subjecting her to one of those rib-bruising embraces?

As she splashed cool water over her face, Aurelia was tormented by words her grandmother had once spoken to her. *Be careful what you wish for, child. It might be granted.* She shook off the disturbing memory as she toweled away the droplets of moisture from her skin. Nay, she was out of sorts this morning because of a surfeit of champagne, not Justin. All her wishes were coming true and she *was* happy. She adored Justin, and he seemed to be devoted to her. What more could she desire? Declining to pursue that question any further, she stood stiff as a statue while Wallis flung a cambric gown of sea-green muslin over her head, then slipped on Roman sandals with crisscross lacing over her silk stockings. Barely giving the maid time to dress her hair, Aurelia trudged out of the bedchamber, not so eager to greet Justin as she was to escape the disconcerting thoughts that lurked in the solitude of her room.

Justin awaited her in Lady Foxcliff's Oriental drawing room. He stared out the bay window, frown lines marring his handsome brow, his hands jammed into the pockets of his beige-colored riding jacket.

When he continued unaware of her presence, she snapped, "Good morning, Justin."

He turned at the sound of her voice, his grim features relaxing into a smile. "Ah, Reely. I mean, Aurelia. Good morning, or perhaps we should say good afternoon."

"Well, if you had not kept me up dancing until all hours, mayhap I would have been ready when you arrived."

"I was not complaining, *ma belle*." Justin crossed over to her side, lifting first one of her hands, then the other, to his lips. Was it her imagination, or was there a certain perfunctoriness in the gesture?

"You look absolutely radiant this morning," he murmured. "Like spring violets newly washed with dew."

Since she felt more like a wilted dandelion, his remark only served to irritate Aurelia. Scowling, she noted that his cravat had gone askew.

"I wish I could return the compliment." She tugged at the linen about his neck, nigh choking him in her efforts to straighten it. "Truly, Justin, how can you go abroad in that careless manner? Everard would never do so."

"So you have informed me any number of times this past week."

"Pray, forgive me. I had no notion my conversation had begun to bore you." She gave the cravat one final sharp tug.

"No, not in the least, my dear. Besides"—he inched closer—"with such tempting lips as yours, the words scarce matter."

Aurelia quickly sidestepped his encircling arms, then glowered at him in total exasperation. What was the matter

113

with him? The Justin she remembered would never have uttered such foolish remarks to her. Could he not be in love and still speak to her in the old comfortable way?

"Why are you here so soon?" she asked.

"I thought I would take you for our drive in St. James's much earlier than yesterday. You grumbled so about all the crush of carriages when we went at five."

"Oh, did I?" Aurelia asked innocently, while inwardly she cringed. She remembered perfectly well complaining that there was hardly any point in going for a promenade in the park. One could scarce see the flowers for the herds of fashionable people trampling down the grass. What was the matter with Justin? she had asked herself. Nay, what was the matter with *her*? She was behaving like an absolute termagant, almost as though she were aching to provoke a quarrel with him. Feeling slightly ashamed of herself, she averted her gaze from Justin and strolled over to an occasional table carved of Jamaican mahogany. She pretended to examine the small tissue-wrapped parcel left lying there. More chocolates. Justin would insist upon bringing her a box of sweetmeats each day, despite the number of times she had begged him to stop. Everard would never have subjected her to such temptation. She suppressed a sigh of self-disgust. Why must she always be comparing the two men?

"I suppose I have not accustomed myself to town ways as yet," she said, turning back to Justin. She could not quite keep a touch of acid from her voice when she added, "When one is left *alone* so much in the country, one develops a penchant for solitude."

Justin replied cheerfully enough. "Aye, 'twould seem that this "penchant" must be contagious. Ev has not been of the most sociable disposition since he returned from Norfolk, either, though I daresay he is too taken up with that new gaming hell, er, establishment that he's found."

114

Gaming hell? The casually dropped words sent a cross-bolt of alarm shooting through Aurelia.

"Is that where he has been spending his time—gaming? And he, already in such difficulties. Justin! You're his friend. How can you permit it?"

Justin gaped at her in astonishment. " 'Tis scarcely my place to interfere if Ev wants to—"

"*He* would if your positions were reversed. Everard would never permit you to ruin yourself."

Justin threw back his head in a hearty laugh. "There's hardly any likelihood of ruin, my sweet, not when you consider the pile of money he's come into."

Aurelia's lips parted to deliver another rebuke, but instead she faltered, "P-pile of money?"

"Aye. 'Twould seem you haven't acquired a knack for town gossip, either. Why, I would have thought Lady Foxcliff would have spoken of it. Ev's poor old *Albatross* came limping into harbor two days ago. The venture was a smashing success. He's now as rich as Midas."

Aurelia slowly sank down upon a cross-legged ottoman. *The Albatross* limped in two days ago? Everard rich, and more important than that, his judgment vindicated. Yet he had never come to tell her about it. Such an important event in his life, and she was left to hear about it by chance. Stark feelings of betrayal slashed through her. Her friend, she thought with bitter scorn of the words, *her dearest friend*.

Her eye fell upon the box of sweetmeats. Of a sudden she seized it, ripping off the lid. Damn you, Everard Ramsey. She began popping the chocolates in her mouth, one after the other, swallowing with difficulty past the knot of tears in her throat.

Justin observed her in bemused astonishment. "There is no need for you to eat in such haste, Reely. We can bring the chocolates with us if you like."

But by the time her maid had fetched her pelisse, and

Justin's tiger brought the high-perched phaeton around, the box was empty. Justin whipped his team of grays in the direction of St. James's. Aurelia sat beside him in glum silence, feeling completely miserable over Everard's defection. As the phaeton's great sprawling wheels rattled past the park's stately line of elms and flourishing lime trees, she scarce heeded Justin's constant stream of remarks. Good Lord, couldn't the man ever sense when one wished to be silent?

"Look, there's old Jack," he said, drawing the phaeton near the pond known as the Long Water. "Queen Charlotte placed him here in St. James's herself. Dreadful nuisance. He's drowned several dogs, to say nothing of pulling a little boy into the water."

Aurelia flicked a desultory glance toward the shimmering blue surface and the elderly man who was feeding a flock of wild ducks at the shore's edge.

"He looks a harmless enough old gentleman to me," she said.

Justin roared with laughter. "You knew I meant that large, rather nasty looking swan, not old Mr. Peterborough." Still chuckling, Justin eased his hand down to squeeze her knee. "Ah, Reely, in some respects, you will never change."

"Nor will you, I fear." She seized his hand and flung it back at him. "Will you kindly stop behaving like a cake and tend to your driving."

His smiling good humor quite vanquished, Justin did as she requested, though she heard him mutter. "Aye, in many respects, you haven't changed. You still behave as though you were my older sister."

Aurelia winced, but she knew she deserved the remark. In truth, she was behaving most unfairly. 'Twas Everard that angered her, with his Turkish treatment of her since they had come to London. One would have thought their friendship would have meant a little more to him than that.

Yet Aurelia was feeling entirely too wretched to apologize to Justin for making him the brunt of her ill-humor.

Instead she said, "Justin, I should like to go home."

"Home? But we just got here—"

"I mean *home* to Aldgate. I have had rather enough of London."

Justin relaxed his concentration upon the avenue ahead long enough to shoot her a glance of complete incredulity. "Enough of London? In the midst of the season?"

"I—I don't belong here. Quite out of my milieu," she said for her own benefit as much as his. Of course, her sudden desire to escape to the security of her own home had nothing to do with Everard's recent callous behavior. Yet her explanation did not satisfy Justin any more than it truly convinced her.

"Hang it all, Reely." He scowled. "We can't go haring back to Norfolk now. 'Tis deadly dull there this time of year."

"But I did promise Clarice to return in time to stand god-mother to her baby."

"Plague take Clarice. Why can't she bring the baby to London? Then we could all—"

"And," Aurelia continued stubbornly, "I would as lief be married at Aldgate Church. I do so detest all these fashionable crowds. I'm sure it would better please your mother to be spared the journey."

Justin's mouth opened as though he meant to argue the point; then he compressed his lips in a taut line. "Whatever you wish, my dear. After all, 'tis *your* wedding."

He said little for the rest of the drive, leaving Aurelia to note with exasperation that Justin still had not outgrown his habit of sulking when he did not get his own way. The only time he smiled was when they chanced upon another carriage. Despite the fact 'twas not the fashionable hour, there were others taking the air in the park, and a goodly number of them ladies. It did not help Aurelia's depressed

117

spirits to note that whilst she might not be inclined to flirt with her betrothed, many other women appeared more than willing to oblige, chief amongst them Lady Sylvie Fitz-hurst.

Her ladyship strolled along the park's green expanse of lawn, twirling her parasol in such a manner as to attract attention. Her face wreathed in smiles when Justin tipped his high-crowned beaver hat in passing. The sultry blonde stood fluttering her handkerchief long after the phaeton rolled out of sight.

"Did you remark how the pair of them were sitting?" Sylvie gloated to her companion. "So stiff and miserable. I declare, something must already be amiss between Justin and his precious Miss Sinclair."

Augustus Snape slunk from behind the shadows of a gnarled elm tree. He shrugged. "A lover's tiff. Nothing so remarkable in that."

"Pooh, I tell you 'tis a favorable sign. I shall have him back soon. You'll see." Lady Sylvie gazed ruefully in the direction of the iron gates through which the phaeton had disappeared. "If only I could have got them to stop. Without Everard Ramsey to intervene, I might have induced that sow to stuff herself upon some of St. James's syllabubs."

Snape's pale eyes regarded her with contempt. "In truth, Lady Sylvie, I had hoped you would conceive of a more clever plan to disrupt Lord Justin's engagement than merely attempting to wreak havoc upon Miss Sinclair's waist-line."

"Well, it's been nigh two weeks since her arrival in London." Sylvie pouted. "I haven't heard you putting forth any scheme of surpassing brillance, either."

"I have been biding my time. Now, I believe, the moment for action approaches. I shall be escorting you to Vauxhall Gardens tomorrow evening."

Sylvie flicked her parasol over her shoulder, staring disdainfully down her nose. "And what, pray tell, makes you think I would be seen at Vauxhall with you?"

"Because Lord Spencer and Miss Sinclair will also be there."

"How in the world do you know that?"

"I have my ways."

Sylvie shrugged. "I still do not see what is to be gained by my spending another evening watching Justin and that—"

"That is because you are so lacking in imagination," Snape purred. His thin lips parted in a secretive smile. "There are so many interesting dark walks at Vauxhall. Anything can happen there, my dear Lady Sylvie. *Absolutely anything.*"

The candles in the silver-carved sconces burned dangerously low, their attempt to dispel the night's shadows from Lady Foxcliff's heavy-velvet-curtained library growing more feeble by the moment. Aurelia thought of ringing for fresh candles, but it seemed hardly worth the effort. Surrounded by four walls of books in the small room, she had as yet to find a volume capable of diverting her unhappy thoughts. Restlessly thumbing row after row of musty leather-bound texts, Aurelia finally settled on a copy of Defoe's *Robinson Crusoe*.

She flopped down upon the comfortable cushions of an overstuffed chesterfield, kicking off her slippers and tucking her stockinged feet beneath the hem of her ancient gray gown. Catching a glimpse of herself in the broad gilt mirror above the fireplace, she took a grim, almost vicious satisfaction in how dreadful she looked. She had promised Everard she would burn the dress. The much-mended dull frock now had a scorch mark on the hem where she had nearly complied. In an agony of nervous apprehension, she had rescued the faded cotton from the flames at the last moment. And a very good thing she had! The somber color not only exactly suited her mood this evening, but 'twould render her most unappealing to any gentleman who might chance to call upon her, especially if that gentleman was prone to study her disdainfully through a quizzing glass.

Not that she expected Everard to call. Apparently 'twas only she that remembered a certain early spring afternoon by the lake shore, his hand pressing hers, murmuring assurances; *If you truly need me, I'll be there.* But that was all before Mr. Everard Ramsey had become a man of wealth and importance. Now he clearly had no time for old friends.

And as for Justin, her beloved had very cheerfully departed for Lady Martingdale's supper party without her. She supposed he was still wounded because of what she had said to him that afternoon. Not that Justin had sulked for long. When they chanced upon Lady Carlisle about to ride her spirited black mare into the park, Justin had reined in the phaeton and immediately begun making a cake of himself over her. Lady Carlisle was so much more receptive and adept at flirting than Aurelia could ever hope to be.

Men! Aurelia thought, turning a page of her book so forcefully she nearly wrenched the paper from its binding. Perfidious creatures, every one of them. Especially ones with waving dark hair and treacherous blue eyes. She sniffed. Robinson Crusoe had no notion how fortunate he was. A desert island populated by no males of any kind sounded a wonderful proposition in her present humor. She would even have driven the faithful Friday into the sea.

A soft knock sounded at the door. For a brief second, Aurelia forgot about the solitary bliss of an island, her heart lurching with sudden hope. After all, one would think that Everard would at least take the time to call upon his aunt.

Her ladyship's butler entered, bearing a small parcel for Aurelia. Aurelia sank deeper into the sofa as she accepted it, her spirits plummeting once more. From the shape of the box she could tell it was only another supply of chocolates sent by Justin.

When the library door had closed behind the manservant, Aurelia halfheartedly examined the accompanying card. It contained Justin's curt wishes that the contents might "sweeten" Aurelia's disposition and render her more reasonable about remaining in London. Sighing, she began tugging at the wrapping strings. So Justin had not completely given up hope of prevailing upon her to . . .

Her lips parted in an "ohh" of astonishment as the lid from the box clattered to the floor. 'Twas not more chocolates. Cradled within a nest of tissue paper was a large pink rose, its petals and green leaves all wrought of glistening sugar. Aurelia stared at the delicately shaped confection, which looked almost too beautiful to eat, an odd sensation of melancholy sweeping over her.

No matter what she might think about Justin's lack of perception, he knew her quite well. Beneath all the fine trim and feathers, she was naught but a little country mouse pining for a nibble of sweets. Was it any wonder Justin was already turning his gaze so blithely toward another lady? Oh, she might have dazzled him briefly, but she was still much the same plain creature she had always been, lacking in all feminine charm. She could almost hear her mother's voice echoing with brittle laughter at Aurelia's folly in imagining she could ever be otherwise.

Feeling more than a little sorry for herself, Aurelia leaned back against the cushions, her book sliding to the floor. At one time in her life, she would have devoured the confection, eagerly seeking consolation in the sweet taste of the sugar dissolving upon her tongue. But, surprisingly, she found she would as soon have set the rose aside. Clutching the confectionary box between her hands, Aurelia wearily closed her eyes.

A wry smile tugged at her lips. She had as yet to taste of the rose, but this was usually the moment she could count upon Everard to rise up before her, as swift and ominous as an avenging spirit summoned by a wizard's spell. She could picture exactly how he would look, the lean contours of his face rigid with disapproval, dark brows arched thunderously over furious blue eyes, his sensitive mouth set into a forbidding line. He would stride forward to snatch—

The floorboards in the library creaked in a manner far too vivid even for her imagination. Aurelia's eyes fluttered open. Garbed in immaculate black evening clothes and frothy white cravat, the object of her fantasy stood glowering over her, his hands pressed against his hips. He looked so much like the image she had conjured up herself only moments before, Aurelia sat up slowly. Cautiously she poked at the vision's exposed wrist. Warm flesh jerked beneath her fingertip.

With a rueful sigh, Aurelia raised her eyes to confront Everard's angry stare. Her hand moved almost reflexively to conceal the sugar rose. How could he possibly always know? There was something not quite natural about the man.

"Are—are you some sort of a warlock?" she croaked.

The hard expression on his face did not waver as he ignored her foolish question. "I did not intend to startle you. Reeves told me where you were, and I knocked at the door before I came in. When you didn't answer, I thought you had fallen asleep."

"Oh no, I wasn't sleeping. I—I—"

" 'Tis quite obvious what you were doing."

"I—I was reading." Aurelia scrambled about looking for her book, then brought herself up short. Why should she always permit Everard to make her feel like a guilty schoolgirl?

A defiant smile hardened her mouth. "And I was just about to partake of this delightful surprise Justin sent me.

122

You know how dreadfully fond I am of roses. Would you care for a piece?"

She extended the box, half expecting Everard would dash it from her hand.

"No, thank you." He flicked the sugar rose a derisive glance before stalking away to lean one arm up against the mantel. The box trembled in Aurelia's fingers as she settled it back upon her lap.

"Pray be seated, Mr. Ramsey," she said. "This is a most unexpected pleasure. Whatever has pulled you away from your cards so early? Did you draw a jester, and it reminded you of me?"

Her forced gaiety was met with silence. Aurelia studied the stone-carved lines of his profile with dismay. He seemed so much farther removed from her than just the width of the room. Had she only imagined that day by the lake when she had felt so close to him, as though she had finally slipped past his elegant facade and drawn nigh to touching the heart of this bewildering, infuriating man? Aye, she must have, for the coolness of his eyes entirely mocked that belief. His gaze swept a disparaging path from her toes peeking out beneath her faded gown to the disheveled auburn curls that she now attempted to brush back from her eyes.

With great difficulty, Everard resisted the urge to rush at Aurelia and shake her. He had just spent a hellish two weeks trying to forget how much he loved this woman. Night after night, gaming until all hours, at the card tables at White's, shooting hazard at a less reputable establishment. What a bitter irony it had been to rise from the tables, a perpetual winner, *now* when all that mattered was the filling of his empty hours.

How he had ached for just one glimpse of Aurelia, to see the way her mouth quivered with laughter, the militant sparkle in her eye when she was about to level him with her wit. Then to find her looking like this! So pathetic, surfeiting her misery upon sweets. And from whence she had dredged up that old gray rag? He should have burned it himself.

He could guess what had inspired such behavior. Playing at whist with Lord Martingdale in his private study, Everard had glimpsed Justin arriving for the supper party, but not with Aurelia upon his arm. Sporting a new set of diamonds that had never come from her clutch-fisted husband, Lady Carlisle had draped herself over Justin in a way that was positively shameful. But Aurelia's response, hiding out here, reverting to her old habits, infuriated Everard as much as Justin's lack of fidelity. When would the woman ever learn she deserved better treatment from her betrothed—but far more important than that, better from herself?

"I met my aunt at Lady Martingdale's, and she told me you were ill." Everard laced his voice with sarcasm. "I can see you are in a worse case than I had feared."

"Not at all. I have never felt better." Her smile over bright, Aurelia broke off a large leaf of the sugar rose and paused, eyeing him. Was she deliberately trying to provoke him? Everard clenched his hands into fists.

"Then why didn't you accompany Justin tonight?" he asked.

"Ennui." She heaved a gusty sigh. "I'm beginning to find these affairs a crashing bore." Slowly, ever so slowly, she began raising the confection to her lips, giving Everard ample opportunity to prevent her.

He forced his hands to relax, folding his arms across his chest. "If you are waiting for me to stop you, Aurelia, you are going to be sadly disappointed. I am no longer interested in acting as your nursemaid."

Although her cheeks reddened, Aurelia defiantly rammed the section of rose in her mouth. She appeared to swallow with great difficulty. "Ummmm, delicious. No, I didn't in the least expect you to keep bothering about me. A man with your important business interests, the untold responsibilities of wealth—''

She paused long enough to break off another piece of the rose. Everard gritted his teeth.

"If I had only known *The Albatross* had come in, I would have sent you a box of chocolates to celebrate. Oh, but, silly me." She laughed hoarsely. "I forgot you don't care for sweets. But I could have eaten them for you if only you had told me."

"It didn't seem important enough," Everard said, even though he remembered how the news had filled him with unspeakable joy. He had rushed to the dockside to gaze upon the tall-masted ship with his own eyes, drink in the sight of her battered hull, her windswept sails. The moment had not been spoiled, until his solicitor, a dry little man who had known Everard since he was in short coats, had coughed and said, "Most miraculous, Master Ramsey. But I hope you do not intend to immediately plunge into another venture of this kind?"

Everard had emitted a happy bark of laughter. "Rest easy, Mr. Quincey. My speculating days are over."

The solicitor had nodded in approval. "Time to settle down on an estate, young sir. Offer your heart to some fortunate lady and set about providing your father with a grandson."

The old man's kindly meant advice had effectively robbed Everard of all delight in *The Albatross's* return, and had brought back the feelings he had been trying to suppress. Aye, he was wealthy enough now to take a bride, but he could not *offer his heart* where it was not wanted, where the fortunate lady in question had already made her choice, and that choice his closest friend.

Everard wrenched his mind back from the bright, sunlit harbor and focused on the wax candles guttering in their silver sconces. The light from the tiny flames flickered over his features, but the glow was not enough to dispel the pale shadows, the careworn lines etched about his eyes. Yet Aurelia was far too caught up in her own unhappiness. She scarce noted the slump of broad shoulders normally carried so gracefully erect. Her throat ached with misery. Was Everard truly going to stand there and permit her to devour the entire rose?

"Not important enough to tell me?" she echoed his description of *The Albatross*. "Your pardon, sir. I have never detained anyone from affairs they consider more important. I am sure at this very moment you have other weightier—"

She nearly jumped from her seat when Ramsey slammed his palm against the mantel and said in a voice taut with control, "Go upstairs and get dressed, Aurelia. I am taking you to Lady Martingdale's. To Justin. Where you belong."

Although her heart was thudding, Aurelia settled back on the sofa with every impression of ease. She forced herself to eat another leaf of the rose, although the cloying sugar coated her tongue, all but sickening her. "I am quite comfortable where I am, Mr. Ramsey."

"While you are being quite comfortable, *Miss Sinclair*, Lady Carlisle and Sylvie Fitzhurst are at this very moment battling over whom your betrothed will take in to supper. I thought you came to London to win Justin's heart, not to sample all the confectionaries."

Aurelia affected a careless shrug. "I scarce see what I could do about the situation. I cannot take on both Lady Carlisle and Lady Silvie. Mayhap when I get more up to my fighting weight—"

Her words broke off in a gasp when Everard charged across the room. Seizing her wrists in a painful grasp, he hauled her to her feet. The box containing the sweetmeat tumbled to the carpet, the rose shattering into myriad sparkling sugar crystals.

"Damn you, Aurelia! I am tired of your sitting around in a corner weeping, feeling sorry for yourself."

She twisted her hands, trying to yank free. "I don't sit in a corner. When I weep, I am quite brazen about it. I do it in the center of the room. Now let me go!"

Fear mingled inside her with a peculiar sensation of triumph in having breached his icy reserve. She had never seen Everard so furious before. His lips were pinched white with his anger, his eyes blazing like blue embers of fire.

"Did you learn nothing about yourself this past winter besides the fine art of self-pity?" he grated. "I suppose the new clothes, the diet, were not enough if you still believe you can be bested by women the likes of Sylvie Fitzhurst. At the first sign of any difficulty, you go diving for a box of chocolates."

"At least, 'tis far less expensive than diving for a deck of cards," she shot back.

For a moment, she thought she detected a flash of pain in his eyes, but 'twas quickly gone, replaced by a furious glint. He gave her a brisk shake. "Don't change the subject. How do you expect Justin or—or anyone else—to care about you when you do not care enough about yourself? You could be a queen, but you persist in acting as though you deserve to be treated like a scullery maid."

Aurelia yanked her hands free with a mighty pull. Retreating a step, she blinked back angry tears. "Mayhap your lessons were incomplete, Mr. Ramsey. You never taught me how to swish my skirts and bat my eyelashes."

Aurelia swept into a mocking curtsy, furiously fluttering her eyes, speaking in a too-sweet falsetto. "Ohh, la, sir. I vow you will quite turn my head with your compliments. I am nigh ready to swoon at your feet."

Everard's mouth clamped into a tight hard line. "I never thought you desired lessons in how to act like a fool."

"But my accomplishments are quite lacking, sir." Aurelia simpered, continuing to goad him. "Why, you never even taught me the proper way to kiss."

The instant the words were spoken Aurelia flushed, regretting them. Her statement seemed to crackle in the air between them, charging the room with a stifling tension. Everard's eyes narrowed to points of steel.

"Then by all means," he said, his voice low, dangerous. "Allow me to complete your education."

Before she could move or cry out in protest, his arms were around her, crushing her against him, the expanse of his chest unyielding beneath the layer of black silk, the frothy lace of his shirt front. His hand shot up, gripping the nape of her neck, forcing her head back. His mouth hovered above hers for the barest instant, before crashing down to claim her lips. Aurelia was too stunned to put up more than a token struggle before she became lost in the bruising, sensual tempest of Everard's kiss.

The stiff awkwardness she had known in Justin's arms quite vanished. Her body swayed against Everard's lean frame, melting to him in a way that was positively shameful. Sparks of fire snapped through her veins. Her struggles ceased altogether, her lips clinging to his, her heart thundering in her ears.

She staggered when Everard thrust her away, breaking the warm contact of his mouth, leaving her feeling bereft. His features ashen, she saw the muscles in his jaw working as he struggled for control.

"Aurelia," he said "I—I don't know what the devil got into me. My abominable temper . . ."

"Oh, no, Everard, please." She flushed to the roots of her hair. " 'Twas—t'was all my fault. I provoked you. I have been behaving like such a fool tonight. Can you ever forgive me?"

"Damn it, Aurelia. Don't you dare apologize. You have every right to be angry. You should slap my face, claw my eyes out."

A quavery laugh escaped her. "I don't want to scratch your eyes out. You would have wasted such a dreadful amount of money on quizzing glasses." Her words coaxed no smile from his lips. He continued to look so stricken with self-reproach, as though his sense of honor had been shaken to the very core, as though he had betrayed—

Justin. The name slammed into Aurelia's consciousness with the impact of a fist driving between her breasts. But all feelings of guilt were entirely overridden by her fear as she observed the strange look settling over Everard's features. He looked like—like some noble highwayman about to place his neck in the noose to compensate for his crimes. She could almost feel him putting distance between them.

"I hope that such a ridiculous quarrel will not spoil our friendship," Aurelia stammered. "Please. Can we not simply forget this ever happened?" She extended her hand toward him in a tentative gesture.

Everard stared out the library window for a moment, the night beyond the latticed panes as dark as the shadowed expression on his face. "Aye, forget," he murmured. He slowly took her hand. Aurelia thought he meant to carry it to his lips, but instead he proffered a wooden handshake. Then he flashed her his odd half smile, bade her good evening and was quickly gone, forgetting to close the door behind him.

Somehow Aurelia's shaking limbs carried her to the portal. She clicked the door shut, leaning heavily against the smooth-grained oak surface. Raising her fingers, she touched her trembling lips, the hot, sweet fury of Everard's mouth still lingering there. Now why couldn't Justin—She tried to shove the treacherous thought aside.

"Aurelia Sinclair loves Justin Spencer. Aurelia Sinclair loves . . ." she repeated, clinging with desperation to the remnants of her childhood dream. Being in love with Justin was such a comfortable prospect. She had known him forever. So convenient.

She winced. Since when had she started thinking of her affection for Justin in such terms as comfortable and convenient?

But 'tis true, whispered a voice inside her that refused to be stilled. What could be more secure than falling in love with a man whom one is already bound to marry? So much safer than launching upon deep, unchartered waters, waters as blue and unfathomable as Everard Ramsey's eyes.

Aurelia pressed her hands to her burning cheeks. No, she could not be that fickle, to be so swayed by one kiss. But it was more than the kiss, she had to acknowledge. It was waltzing in a pair of strong arms that knew just how to hold her. It was the scolding, the badgering, the caring, that had forced her to bring forth the best in herself. It was the shared laughter, the moments of companionable silence, when there had been no need for words.

Stumbling across the room, she stooped to gather up the remains of the broken rose. But the pent-up emotion, the tears she had denied for so long, refused to be contained. They overflowed, splashing down her cheeks, one crystal droplet dissolving the particles of sugar in her hand.

What an idiot she was. Five long years she had had to think before becoming engaged. And now! Now, when it was far too late, she discovered she had betrothed herself to the wrong man.

Chapter 8

Everard linked his arm through Lady Foxcliff's, impatiently threading his way through the throng of happy fools meandering along Vauxhall Garden's Grand Walk. The avenue shimmered with a thousand colored lanterns rivaling the glow of the starlit spring sky; the crisp night air was adrift with the hush of rustling leaves, the gurgle of the fountains, and the lilting music of violins.

Everard attempted to block out the babble of mirthful voices. The gay sounds were an affront to his dark mood and the dull ache in his heart, as he reminded himself over and over that he could never see Aurelia again.

"Don't look so glum, Nevvy," Lady Foxcliff said, her almost masculine stride kicking up the gravel as they passed under one of the triumphal arches bestriding the path. "Smile, man. Enjoy yourself. After all, 'tis your last night in London. Though why you are in such a hurry to go haring off is beyond me."

"Business," Everard said curtly. "I should have been gone long since." Aye, gone long before anything like that kiss ever happened. He cursed himself silently. Why hadn't he followed through on the resolve he had formed when he first realized he loved Aurelia? To stay away from her, to drive this hopeless passion from his heart. But both were

131

equally impossible as long as he remained in England, continued to walk the same shores that she—

"Ramsey!"

Everard drew in a sharp breath as his aunt's fan whacked him on the knuckles. "Mind your steps. You nigh plastered my nose against that fellow's loincloth."

Everard snapped back to his surroundings long enough to stare up at a towering figure of Apollo, his bulging white biceps and disdainful stone eyes seeming to dare all mortals to set one foot off the walkway into his private glade.

"Sorry," Everard muttered, guiding his aunt back onto the gravel path.

"I declare." The feathers on Lady Foxcliff's gold silk turban shook vehmently. "Much more of these wool-gathering looks and I'll be getting the impression you don't want to have a bite of sup with your poor old auntie."

Everard shot a wry glance at the tall woman whose strapping shoulders rivaled his own, but he said politely. "Not at all, Aunt Lydia. There is no one I would rather be with."

"Hah, Liar!" Lady Foxcliff's eyes narrowed, an expression of shrewdness lurking in their depths that Everard found annoying.

" 'Tis only that I do not understand why we had to come to Vauxhall," he continued. Raising his quizzing glass, he studied the crowd. Rowdy shop clerks bumped elbows with even more boisterous noblemen. A shameless lightskirt squealed, plunging down one of the narrower dark paths, pursued by a leering gent Everard recognized from one of his gaming halls.

"This place is too vulgar by half."

Lady Foxcliff halted in her tracks. "Stuff and nonsense." 'Tis exceedingly romantic. This is where I proposed, er, where my first husband asked me to marry him."

She sighed gustily at the memory. "Of course, it created the most dreadful scandal. You see, *I was already be-*

trothed to Lord Wyburton at the time. But when one falls in love, all other considerations seem of no importance.''

"Indeed," Everard said glumly. How well he knew the truth of that.

"Don't you agree with me, Nevvy?"

"Agree?" Everard repeated blankly.

"Aye!" Her ladyship stamped her foot. "Don't you think 'tis better to have the scandal of a broken engagement rather than condemn two—mayhap—three people to a lifetime of misery?"

Although ashamed of his inattentiveness, Everard shrugged. He was in little humor to listen to Aunt Lydia's reminiscences about her long-dead husbands, but he tried to frame a suitable response. "There are always questions of honor to be weighed—"

"Bah!" The ostrich feathers quivered as her ladyship gave him a glance of withering scorn. "Exactly like you to have such crack-brained notions rattling in your head. I feared as much.

"And pay attention!" Lady Foxcliff dealt him a sharp rap on the shoulder. "I've no objection to you ogling the Cyprians. 'Tis something you men can't seem to help. But for heaven's sake, show a little discretion."

Everard started, realizing for the first time that while he had been attempting to sort out his aunt's disjointed conversation, he had been staring absently at a buxom blonde mincing her way toward the curving sweep of the supper boxes set within one of the groves. He stiffened when Lady Sylvie Fitzhurst waggled two gloved fingers at him by way of greeting, her lips parting in a sly smile. She walked arm in arm with that bony, slick-haired fellow whose appearance had so disconcerted Aurelia at the Carlisle ball.

"Who is that? My lady Sylvie?" Lady Foxcliff snorted. "She's certainly come down a peg, being seen with that Snape fellow. Rum customer, if there ever was one. Course she ain't much better. Always puts me in mind of a mountain valley."

Scowling, Everard barely acknowledged Lady Sylvie's and Snape's pointed stares. "A valley, Aunt Lydia?"

"Aye, her gowns dip down so low, 'tisn't difficult to get a good view of the peaks."

A reluctant laugh escaped Everard when he guessed from the sudden firing of Lady Sylvie's cheeks that his aunt's booming voice must have carried.

He raised Lady Foxcliff's hand affectionately to his lips. "Aunt Lydia, you truly are the most outrageous old woman. I vow you even put me to the blush sometimes."

Her ladyship gave his fingers a crushing squeeze. "I'll do more than that, sir, if you give me more trouble about who is to pay the shot for supper this evening. This is to be my treat. Don't care if you have become a nabob."

Her feathers seemed to tremble with proud satisfaction. "Besides, I still insist that I owe you the money on our wager over Reely. After all you won fair and square, working so hard, badgering the poor girl until you turned her into such a belle."

Everard quickly shushed his aunt, his smile fading. He would not find it amusing if Lady Sylvie or anyone else were to overhear that. Even the hint that such a wager had ever existed would stir no end of gossip, cause Aurelia a deal of embarrassment. He noted with relief that Lady Sylvie and her companion had moved on, disappearing behind one of the colonnades that depicted the ruins of Palmyra.

"Well, Aunt Lydia," he said with forced cheerfulness, turning back to her ladyship, determined to make up for his previous ungracious behavior. "Are you ready to assay some of Vauxhall's famous ham?"

"Aye, I am ready to drop in my tracks for want of food. And a large quantity of rack punch, too."

But despite her ladyship's claims of near starvation, she showed a perverse tendency to linger, studying the occupants of the small covered dining areas. When Everard impatiently tried to steer her toward their own supper box, she balked. "Don't be in such a dratted haste. Can't come to Vauxhall and snub all of one's acquaintances."

Everard resisted the urge to fling up his hands in exasperation. Aunt Lydia was being damnably difficult this evening, insisting on dining at Vauxhall, asking him peculiar questions, behaving in a manner that seemed far too whimsical for her usual forthright nature. Her expression was oddly eager, yet at the same time almost secretive.

He was at a loss to account for it until they passed one of the supper boxes situated near the end of the grove. A small oil lamp illuminated the faces of the young couple lingering over their supper. A couple remarkable for the fact that in the midst of all the gaiety and romance surrounding them, they sat a distance apart, looking extremely morose.

But the lady would have been remarkable in any case, Everard thought, experiencing a sudden pang near the region of his heart. Aurelia's loosely-dressed auburn tresses hung freely about her shoulders, satiny waves cascading against the snowy whiteness of neck. Her long, dark lashes spilled against her pale cheeks; her delicate mouth and jawline were so lacking in animation she might have been a portrait instead of the vivacious woman whose sparkling green eyes had captured Everard's heart. Her high-waisted gown of daffodil silk clung to the gentle curves of her breasts in such a way as to stir Everard's senses, despite how manfully he tried to suppress his feelings.

"Damme," he muttered under his breath. He forced his gaze to shift to Justin. Lord Spencer's mouth drooped with what Everard had always termed his "hangdog" look. Everard had seen the same martyred expression a dozen times when his friend had been forced to attend one of his mother's afternoon teas. The only time Justin's slumped shoulders perked to attention was when another set of skirts happened to rustle by the supper box.

A bitter surge of anger washed through Everard. Blast Justin! How could he be so blind, gazing at other women, when Aurelia sat only a heartbeat away, the velvet texture of her lips positively begging to be kissed. The fool didn't appreciate what love was his for the asking, didn't deserve to wed Aurelia.

Everard ground his fingers against his temples, appalled at the direction his thoughts were taking. Nay, he was simply trying to find excuses for his own selfish wishes. For, in truth, it mattered naught whether Justin deserved Aurelia or no. She loved him, Everard reminded himself hollowly. *She loved him.*

Tugging on his aunt's arm, he tried to melt back into the line of trees before Aurelia or Justin looked around. Much to his dismay, Lady Foxcliff broke free of his grasp and strode forward, hallooing in a voice loud enough to capture the attention of half the grove.

"Justin! Reely!"

Everard had no choice but to steel his features into what he hoped was his customary expression of cynicism and trail after her ladyship. Justin leaped up at their approach, appearing glad of any diversion, but Aurelia dove beneath the folds of a China crepe shawl, looking very much as though she wanted to pull it over her head.

"Well, I declare." Lady Foxcliff beamed as she pushed her way through the door at the back of the supper box. "Such a pleasant surprise!"

"Surprise?" Justin echoed. "But you gave me permission to bring Reely to—oofff." He broke off with a pained gasp as her ladyship's elbow found the tender part of his stomach.

"Everard and I were just strolling the grounds, merry as grigs," she continued, "when I said to him, 'now doesn't that look like Justin and Aurelia over there?' "

"Yes, doesn't it?" Everard repeated dryly. He began to eye his aunt with dawning suspicion. All her irrevelant chatter about broken engagements and love being worth the scandal began to make sense. While knowing that Aunt Lydia's meddling must be inspired by her affection for him, Everard was not about to permit her ladyship to ride rough-shod over Aurelia's feelings.

Aurelia rose shakily to her feet. Everard was painfully aware that she avoided glancing in his direction. So much for her brave little speech about forgetting the insult he had offered her last night. A rush of emotion swept through him—love, tenderness, despair—all of which he hoped his countenance did not reveal.

"Justin and I had just begun our supper. Won't you join us?" Aurelia congratulated herself that she managed to extend the invitation without her voice squeaking. She half hoped, half feared Everard would decline, but he scarce had any say in the matter. Lady Foxcliff leaped at the suggestion with alacrity, settling herself next to Justin.

With perfect gallantry, Everard held Aurelia's chair for her while she reseated herself. She fixed her gaze upon her plate, not daring to let him see into her eyes. One look and he would know she had spent half the night sniffing into her pillow, resolving that Everard should never be burdened with the knowledge she had fallen in love with him.

He eased himself into the chair beside her, taking care not to brush against her skirts. Aurelia could not refrain from stealing one glance at his face. How embarrassed he looked. How uncomfortable. *She had done this to him.* The kiss that had awakened her to these feelings of love had destroyed something very precious. They could never be friends again.

She could read that in the rigid line of his mouth . . . the same mouth that had moved over hers in such demanding fashion, stirring such flames, the same flames which

137

now flared into her cheeks until she felt her flesh must burn more hotly than one of the garden's lanterns.

Aurelia snatched up a napkin, fanning herself. If she did not stop this, she would never be able to behave naturally with him. She would have them all staring at her.

"Are you not hungry, Everard?" she croaked when he made no move to fill his plate. "The—the food is excellent." Her gaze traveled involuntarily back to the warm curve of his mouth. "You should try the chicken lips. I—I mean the thighs," she stammered, her eyes locking on the lean musculature of his legs, outlined by the tight-fitting silk breeches.

"Would you like some ham?" she finished, blushing more hotly than ever. This was absurd. She had fought and jested with this man all winter; now she was behaving like a perfect widgeon.

"No, thank you."

Was that a note of disgust she heard in his voice? Nay, he only sounded weary, so unutterably sad that she longed to reach out to him and—

Aurelia caught herself before she'd actually touched his sleeve. Grabbing up her fork, she attacked a wafer-thin slice of ham.

"Pig's already dead, Reely," Justin's jovial tones carried across the table. It was one of the few comments he had volunteered all evening. Aurelia glared at him. For someone who had appeared so glum only moments ago, he was looking unaccountably merry.

But the retort she had been about to utter died on her lips. How could she even think of rebuking Justin, when she sat here at his table, betraying him in her heart. Overcome with guilt, Aurelia permitted her fork to clatter into her plate, lapsing into a silence as deep and painful as Everard's.

All conversation was left to Justin and Lady Foxcliff, which they managed with a rollicking good humor, making

Aurelia long to gag them both. The pair of them chattered and laughed, all the while stewing their own chicken in a china dish over the lamp in such boisterous fashion, Aurelia thought it was a mercy they did not set the supper box afire. She felt considerably relieved when the meal had ended and her ladyship suggested they stroll toward the orchestra rotunda to hear the new singer.

"For I simply dote on music," Lady Foxcliff said, addressing her remarks principally to Justin. "I always say there's no finer way to pass an evening than watching some great fat dame shaking like a blancmange, caterwauling out some tunes by that Handey fellow."

"Handel," Everard said wearily. "Aunt Lydia, I don't think—"

But Justin jumped up eagerly. "That's a capital notion. I'm dashed fond of 'Handey' myself. What a great gun he was for churning out those ditties."

The next instant Lady Foxcliff had linked her arm through Justin's, and the pair of them charged off down the lantern-lit pathway with as much enthusiasm as though they were bound for a race meeting.

An awkward silence ensued. For the first time that evening Aurelia raised her head, daring to meet Everard's eyes. Although he was looking slightly vexed, his mouth twitched as he struggled in vain to maintain his gravity.

"Well, Aunt Lydia's tastes in music have taken a most surprising turn. She once vowed to me the sweetest melody she'd ever heard was the braying of her hounds when they'd run a fox to the ground."

Aurelia's own mouth began to quiver. "A-aye, and I'd always believed that Justin's entire range of musical experience consisted of the time he severed the strings in his sister's pianoforte so that she was unable to practice."

Everard's deep chuckle swelled into a laugh, a laugh that Aurelia heard her own voice echoing. She felt some of the constraint between them beginning to dissolve. How good it felt to be able to laugh with Everard again. Like a burst of sunshine after a dreary drizzling rain. Mayhap there was hope after all. But what she hoped for Aurelia scarce dared allow herself to think.

"I'd expect we'd best hasten after them," Everard said. "I don't know whether Madame Vivani will be quite braced to find two such enthusiastic admirers amongst her audience."

He reached for her arm. "In any case, it will put us in an excellent position for when the fireworks begin."

As his strong, tapering fingers skimmed the sensitive underside of her arm, Aurelia felt as though the fireworks had already begun. The warm pressure of his hand next to her flesh seemed to set a skyrocket bursting inside her.

Fretting the ends of her shawl to disguise the tremor that shot through her, she permitted Everard to escort her from the supper box. Deeply conscious of his broad, well-formed shoulder brushing so close to hers with every step, Aurelia stared down at the ground as though nothing were more fascinating than the stride of his boots across the gravel. His every movement seemed the very embodiment of masculine grace.

She stifled a sigh. If only she had met Everard sooner . . . Then what? a mocking voice inside her cried. Did she dare to presume that such a connoisseur of feminine beauty, such a stickler for perfection, would ever have cherished a tendre for her? She, whom all the silks and jewels in the world could not transform into anything other than the plain, awkward creature that she was, let alone the sort of elegant lady that Ramsey would be able to love.

Caught up in her grim self-disparagement, Aurelia did not see the skeletal form of Augustus Snape approaching until it was too late. Lurking in the shelter of one of the arches, he fairly leaped out at her like some scrawny cat about to pounce upon its prey, his pale-colored eyes narrowed with malevolence.

Dismayed, Aurelia halted in her tracks. She had been dreading such a confrontation ever since the night of the Carlisle ball. She only wondered what had taken Snape so long.

"Good evening, Miss Sinclair. I have been looking for you. So distressed to think of you being left all alone in the middle of Vauxhall Gardens." An oily smile bedecked Snape's ferretlike features.

Before Aurelia could muster her startled wits to make reply, Everard asked sharply, "And pray tell, sir, why would you expect to find Miss Sinclair unescorted?" He leveled his quizzing glass at Snape, conveying the impression that some new and highly undesirable species of reptile had just slithered from the bushes.

Snape purpled beneath Everard's stare, his tongue snaking nervously across his lips. He straightened, making a visible effort to recover his manner of sly insolence. "But of course, my dear, I should have realized you would waste little time finding another to take Lord Spencer's place."

"What the deuce do you—" Everard began, but Aurelia hastily interposed herself between the two men.

"In fact, we were just going to look for Lord Spencer. If you will excuse us, sir." She tugged at Everard's arm, which suddenly felt as rigid as though carved of stone.

"No great rush, Aurelia," Everard said. "I believe 'tis time I made this *gentleman's* acquaintance."

The words were spoken pleasantly enough, but when Aurelia glanced up at Everard's face, her heart turned over in alarm. His eyes bore the look of flint striking steel.

"Oh, n-no. Some other time, perchance. I could not bear it if—Good evening, Mr. Snape."

She yanked at Everard's hand, dragging him off the Grand Walk toward one of the darker, less frequented paths, scarce pausing to see if Snape dared follow them. Everard voiced a faint protest, but Aurelia took to her heels, frantically pulling at his hand. Low-hanging branches

141

slapped at her face, tugged at her skirts, but still she refused to stop, determined that Everard should not be put to any further trouble because of her.

When he finally caught both of her arms, forcing her to a standstill, they had come some ways in from the main path and were now well entangled in a maze of dark lanes where the bright glare of the lanterns did not seem to penetrate.

"Hold, Aurelia." Everard panted. "Good Lord, woman, we've come far enough to outdistance the devil."

Aurelia drew in a deep breath, trying to still her pounding heart. Everard's hands lingered upon her shoulders, slowly kneading her tensed muscles beneath the shawl. "Why did you bolt like that? Who *is* that blackguard."

"Snape is—is merely an unpleasant man I once snubbed back in Aldgate. But you looked so fierce. I did not want any sort of embarrassing scene."

"I'm not Justin." The words came low, clipped.

"I know," she whispered sadly. How painfully aware of that fact she was.

"What I mean is," he chided her gently, "don't you know I would never do anything to cause you distress?"

Aurelia hung her head, her panic subsiding. "I—I am sorry," she faltered. "You must think me half mad, dragging you off like that."

His rich chuckle sounded in her ear. "Not at all. In fact, if I had known 'twas the custom for beautiful women to pull gentlemen off into the bushes, I would have visited Vauxhall more often."

Aurelia felt the heat rise into her cheeks and was glad of the concealing night shadows. She became suddenly conscious of how very much alone she was with Everard and how very close he was standing.

" 'Tis exceeding poorly lit in this part of the gardens," she said.

"Aye." His voice had suddenly turned husky. "The

Dark Walk is not one of the more respectable areas of Vauxhall. A place fit only for rogues—and lovers.''

"I suppose we must fit into the former category."

Aurelia meant to sound light, but her words came out scarce above a whisper. She began to wonder about the way Everard had kissed her last night. Mayhap she had but imagined most of his effect upon her. There was no point in her being this miserable if she were not sure she was hopelessly in love with him. If he would only repeat the gesture again . . .

Scarce thinking, she tipped her head back. Everard's shadowed-skimmed features swam before her, his eyes as distant and mysterious as the starlight peering between the tree limbs. His hands trailed slowly down the length of her arms until he caught her fingertips in a firm warm clasp.

"Aurelia. There is something I must say to you."

"Yes?" she asked breathlessly, her heart bounding with wild, impossible desires.

His dark head bent forward as he began to raise her hands to his lips, the vulgar glare of her engagement ring not dimmed even by the pale moonlight. Everard froze, then released her with such a sudden, almost violent movement, Aurelia stumbled backward.

"I am going away." he said, as though the words were wrung from him.

Going away? Aurelia drew her trembling fingers beneath the security of her shawl.

"You—you mean you are going home to see your family?"

"No. I have arranged to set sail upon *The New Wind* tomorrow. To check out some new investment opportunities firsthand in—in Jamaica."

"Jamaica!" To Aurelia, it sounded like the ends of the earth. "You c-could be gone years."

"Very likely. If I like it well enough, I . . ." Everard paused. Turning away from her, he snapped a silver-tipped oak leaf from a low-hanging branch, then continued in a voice which was almost inaudible. "I may not return to England at all."

Aurelia huddled deeper within her shawl. She watched numbly as his graceful fingers shredded the leaf to bits. "So, you see, I will be finally realizing my wish to become a sailor, and you will be marrying Justin. We shall both realize our childhood dreams."

Aurelia could not find her voice to reply. Aye, but dreams had a sad way of changing, shifting so that they were still forever tantalizingly out of reach.

"Were you not even going to come bid me farewell?" she asked.

"I thought after what happened that—" He broke off suddenly at the crackling of twigs underfoot and the murmuring of other voices. Even through her haze of misery, Aurelia noted the way Everard's shoulders stiffened. He parted one of the branches, peering into the distance, the set of his mouth going white, hard. Whirling on his heel, he caught Aurelia by the elbow.

"This is no place for you. We'd best be getting back. Lady Foxcliff will be worried."

He began pulling her from the secluded glade, but Aurelia hung back, listening. "But—but Everard, that sounds like . . ."

"No, it's not Justin!" he snapped. "You are mistaken. Now come with—"

Aurelia wrenched her body around, craning her neck in an effort to peer through the line of trees. Despite all of Everard's efforts to block her view, she caught a glimpse of another couple. The man was undoubtably Justin, and the woman draped all over him was Lady Sylvie Fitzhurst. Justin's hands spanned the waistline of her ladyship's thin gown, while Lady Sylvie hung about his neck, crushing her mouth against his as though she would devour him.

"Oh." Aurelia said softly, though, deep down, she

found she was not all that surprised. But she did feel very much a fool being witness to such a scene, knowing that Everard was regarding her with pity. She ought to be crushed, finding her betrothed in the arms of another woman. Yet, in truth, she did not care a jot. Now if it had been Everard . . . Sharp pangs of jealousy gnawed her at the mere thought, which was completely absurd, considering he was not hers to be jealous of. After tomorrow, she would never even see him again.

Suddenly she was overwhelmed by the painful knowledge. In another moment, she would be bursting into tears.

"I—I should like it very much if we could find Lady Foxcliff. Indeed, I am not feeling quite the thing."

Everard nodded and hastened to escort her back to the Grand Walk. He was grimly silent most of the time, although right before they located Lady Foxcliff by the music pavilion, he made an attempt to assure her everything would be all right. Aurelia scarce heeded his words, concentrating all her will on avoiding a bout of hysterics in the midst of the crowd at Vauxhall Gardens.

Lady Foxcliff looked less than pleased when Everard pulled her away from a very agreeable flirtation she had struck up with an elderly gentleman of her acquaintance.

"Reely wants to leave now? But we shall miss the fireworks. And what of Justin? That ridiculous Mr. Snape came rushing up awhile ago, howling that Sylvie Fitzhurst is missing. Justin went to help look for the blasted wench, and now he's gone and lost himself somewhere."

"You look after Aurelia." Everard ground out. "I will deal with Lord Spencer."

Justin deeply regretted he had ever agreed to help Augustus Snape discover Sylvie's whereabouts, but it had seemed an excellent notion at the time. Not that he had ever shared Snape's apprehension that his former mistress was in any sort of danger, but any activity seemed preferable to listening to Madame Vivani screeching fit to break a man's eardrums.

However he had never expected Sylvie to pounce upon him out of the darkness, then cling like a lymphet. Ardent kisses he'd once found exciting were now downright embarrassing. Eyes seemed to peer at them from behind every bush, and once he was almost certain they'd been spotted. He had to get away from this lunatic female. Faith, she was even attempting to undo his waistcoat buttons, without the slightest concern who might come upon them.

"See here, Sylvie," he spluttered.

"Oh, Justin," she crooned, grinding her bosom against his chest. "It has been forever since we were alone together. I know you have been longing for this as much as I."

"But dash it all, Sylvie. No, don't do that! Someone is coming!"

He tried to thrust her away as two drunken sailors staggered past on a nearby path.

"Eh, look there, Fred. It's a gent in distress. That 'er gel looks fit to rape 'im."

"Be happy to save yer virtue, m'lord. Just send that hot wench over here."

Justin groaned, feeling himself turn red. He pulled Sylvie back farther into the trees until the sailors staggered on their way, their coarse laughter ringing in his ears. Shaking loose from Lady Sylvie, Justin attempted to make a dash back to the Grand Walk. But he had not gone far, when Sylvie was upon him again, pressing hot, moist kisses all over his cheeks.

"Damn, Sylvie, you must stop this. Oh, Lord, I think someone else is walking this way."

"Where?" Sylvie asked. Still clinging to him, she peered eagerly behind her. Blast it, one would think the silly wench wanted to make an exhibition of herself. Everard had warned him this one would cause him trouble.

"I don't see anyone." Sylvie pouted, nestling closer. "Besides, what do you care if she—I mean whoever—sees? Isn't it about time we put an end to all pretense?"

"Pretense?" Justin frowned, trying to salvage the remains of his cravat from her groping fingers. "Sylvie, please. My mother will have my head if I create any sort of a scandal this close to the wedding."

"Aye, that is exactly what I am talking about—your engagement to that little country nobody. You cannot seriously be intending to go through with it."

"Well, I . . ." Damnation! Sylvie was behaving like a madwoman, easing the fabric of her bodice lower across her ample bosom. In another moment—Justin made a frantic grab for the silk, awkwardly trying to halt its downward slide. Sylvie buried her hands in his hair, trying to draw his lips downward toward her exposed flesh.

"Sylvie! Will you please—Now, stop it and help me with this dress."

"I never knew you to require such assistance before." The cold, clipped male voice seemed to cut through the darkness, startling Justin like the slash of a hickory switch. Sylvie relaxed her hold enough for him look up at Everard. Justin had never congratulated himself that he was good at reading other people's expressions, but he could tell that Everard was definitely not amused. In fact, angry seemed too mild a word for the look of accusing fury twisting Ramsey's normally impassive features.

Justin became acutely aware of his disheveled cravat, his hand gripping the front of Sylvie's bodice.

"Damn it, Ev, I know how bad this looks, but I swear to you, for perhaps the first time in my life, I'm innocent. Sylvie, tell him—"

Justin never got to finish his appeal before Everard's fist cracked into his jaw with bone-shattering force. The sound of Sylvie's piercing shriek mingled with that of renting silk. The bodice ripped away in Justin's hand as he went flying backward to land with a dull thud in the dirt.

He sat up slowly, raising one hand in wonderment to his swelling jawline, then stared at Everard, a dazed expression in his eyes. Everard rubbed his throbbing knuckles, a little stunned and even more appalled by his own action. Only months ago, he would have judged himself incapable of such barbarism. Yet he had but to remember the agony on Aurelia's face when she'd glimpsed Justin kissing this witch, and fury surged through Everard anew. Both his hands knotted into fists.

"Damn you, Justin," he hissed. "You shall never serve Aurelia such a trick as this again, not if I have to flay you alive to prevent it."

But as he took a menacing step in his friend's direction, Justin made no move to defend himself. He sat grinning up at Everard like the village idiot.

"Stap me, Ev," he gasped in awed tones. "Who'd ever have imagined *you* to have such a punishing left?"

Before Everard could demonstrate what his right was capable of as well, another male voice called out, "What the deuce is toward here?" Branches thrashed as Augustus Snape's gangly form fought its way into the clearing. He gaped from Everard down to the sprawled limbs of Lord Spencer.

"I believe these two gentlemen are fighting over me," Lady Sylvie smirked, clutching the remnants of her torn bodice. But the simper on her face disappeared at one murderous glance from Everard. She skittered over to hide behind Snape.

"Tut, tut, Mr. Ramsey." Snape's lips pursed with sneering disapproval. "Such uncivilized behavior. And you a gentleman of supposed refinement."

"Go to the devil," Everard snarled. Turning his back on both Snape and Sylvie, he seized Justin by the collar, hauling him to his feet.

148

"Damn, Ev . . . choking me," Justin said, struggling to get free. "No need for . . . no harm done."

"No harm done!" Everard gave Justin such a savage shake, Lord Spencer's teeth clattered together. "You damned fool. *She saw you.* Aurelia saw you fondling that whey-faced trollop."

Lady Sylvie's delighted trill of laughter quickly changed to a gasp of outrage. "How dare you," she shrieked, rushing over to thrust her angry red face within inches of Everard's and the wriggling Justin's. "I am not whey-faced. I mean, I am not a trollop. Ohhhh, Justin, Mr. Snape. Will you permit this varlet to insult me so?"

"Madam, you have exactly two minutes to remove yourself from my sight." Everard tightened his grip on the back of Lord Spencer's neck, totally ignoring Justin's outcry of "Ouch! Damn." "Or," he continued, eyeing her with loathing, "not that there is any question of you being a lady, but I may well forget you are a woman."

Sylvie Fitzhurst's eyes spit venom, but 'twas Augustus Snape who answered for her. Strolling over to the furious woman's side, he said, "Mr. Ramsey! I really must protest."

As Everard glowered at the pair of them, a sudden thought clicked into his mind. Strange . . . exceedingly strange that Snape, the man whose presence so disquieted Aurelia, should be the one to have sent Justin looking for Lady Sylvie. Stranger still that Snape had appeared to know exactly where Justin and Lady Sylvie were to be found. Everard's eyes narrowed. He began to smell something deuced rotten about this entire business, other than the heavy odor of Lady Sylvie's perfume.

He released Justin so abruptly, Lord Spencer all but fell to his knees.

"And what is your interest in this affair, Mr. Snape?" Everard demanded.

Snape ran his thumbs beneath his jacket lapel, thrusting

forward his thin chest like a bantam rooster. "Justice, sir. Besides being a good friend of Lady Sylvie's, I deplore hypocrisy. You are in no position to be chastising Lord Spencer or anyone else. Didn't I see you slipping off into the bushes with Lord Spencer's intended?"

"What, the virtuous Miss Sinclair?" Sylvie chortled with glee.

"The devil you say!" Justin cut in. "Everard would never! Nor Reely either."

Consciousness of his own guilt rendered Everard momentarily speechless as Justin added hotly, "Especially not Reely, no matter how she happened to feel. She's the most perfect lady I ever knew."

Snape sneered. "It pains me to disillusion you, sir. How little you know about your betrothed."

"And you, sir, claim to know the lady better?" The softness of Everard's voice masked all the barely leashed fury roiling beneath the surface.

"Oh prodigiously better. The lady and I spent a great deal of time together in Norfolk. We become intimate friends, most intimate."

"Why, you—" Justin gasped. Everard sensed he was about to lunge, but he moved more quickly than Lord Spencer, dealing several open-handed slaps across Snape's gaunt cheeks. The man staggered backward, his eyes watering.

"You villain," Sylvie shrieked at Everard. "You shall meet Augustus for this."

"N-no, he shan't" Snape gasped, regaining his balance. "Things—getting out of control. My—my apologies. All a jest, sir, about Miss Sinclair."

"Coward! You *will* meet me," Everard said, cracking the back of his hand across Snape's mouth again, until a thin smear of blood appeared. "Unless you desire to be beaten insensible here and now."

Justin thrust himself in front of Everard, his eyes round-ing in alarm. "Now, Ev, this has gone far enough. I'll admit he is a smarmy-faced little weasel but—"

Everard shoved Justin aside, his gaze never wavering from Snape. "My second will wait upon yours at your earliest convenience, sir."

"He accepts," Sylvie hissed, "with pleasure."

What little blood he possessed drained from Snape's countenance. "Shut up, you silly doxy. This was no part of my plan."

"You have but to name who will act for you," Everard continued inexorably, "And your choice of weapons."

"Pistols," Sylvie blurted, her eyes gleaming with vicious satisfaction. "He wants pistols."

"Be quiet, Sylvie," Justin shouted. "Who made you Snape's blasted second?"

"Pistols will be entirely satisfactory," Everard said, his lips tightening.

"Have you run mad?" Justin yelped. "Now I want everyone to calm down and—"

But Everard did not pause for the rest of Justin's frantic speech. He sketched Snape a brief, ironic bow before striding from the clearing. The fury that had driven him to act in a manner so unlike himself slowly drained, leaving him feeling empty and hollow as a well. He smoothed down his coat sleeves, attempting to regain his aura of detachment, which had always served him so well in the past.

Footsteps rustled behind him, but he did not turn around, not even when Justin seized him by the arm.

"Ev, what the devil has gotten into you? You cannot seriously mean to fight Augustus Snape. Why, the little rotter is not even a gentleman. Besides, you know 'tis me you really want to murder."

Everard shrugged. "Mayhap that is so, but 'tis excessively ill-bred to kill one's friends, no matter what the provocation."

Lord Spencer did not return his wry smile. Beads of

151

sweat stood out upon Justin's forehead, and he looked more agitated than Everard would ever have thought possible.

"But—but pistols!" he moaned. "You know Sylvie deliberately primed Snape to choose those. Everyone knows what a bad shot you are. Why, with your notions of honor, Alvaney and Montmorten have had a long-standing bet at the club as to whether you would die being shot in a duel or by a curricle accident."

"How gratifying," Everard drawled, "to be the object of such kindly interest."

He and Justin both started at the sound of a loud report. Overhead, Roman candles suddenly exploded. Everard tipped back his head, staring at the shower of sparks spilling across the inky night sky. He slowly hunched his shoulders. A bullet through his head or a slow, lingering voyage taking him farther and farther from Aurelia. What odds did it make?

Chapter 9

It had taken Aurelia the better part of a sleepless night to reach her decision, most of the morning to summon the courage to act upon it. Facing Justin across the palatial-like crimson-and-gold salon at Spencer House, she squared her shoulders against the stiffly ornate back of the Louis XIV chair.

"Justin, I—I have come here this morning to—to tell you that I cannot marry you."

To Aurelia, it seemed as though her low-spoken words echoed off the gilt ribbing of the high coved ceiling. She waited nervously for Lord Spencer's reaction. Poor Justin was looking decidedly haggard already, as though he had not slept much, either. His brow, normally as untroubled as a babe's, crinkled with deep lines of anxiety; his mischievous gray eyes were dulled by the shadows cast beneath them. An enormous bruise purpled one cheek, making Aurelia wonder what sort of carousing Justin had been engaged in after she left him last night. But despite his disreputable appearance, after she had explained the purpose of her visit, his face brightened, the grim set of his mouth relaxing into a broad grin.

"Try not to be too devastated," she said tartly. "If you continue to look so brokenhearted, I shall be quite overcome with remorse."

His grin erupted into a laugh. "This is wonderful, though not entirely unexpected. I only trust it may not be too late."

Aurelia scarce gave more than a moment's consideration as to what on earth Justin meant. She felt far too annoyed with his lighthearted acceptance of a decision that had cost her a great deal of agonizing. The breaking of an engagement was no small matter, even if it did not involve the breaking of Justin's heart. She was setting aside the plans of both their families, a promise made and accepted in good faith. It was more than slightly dishonorable, in her opinion. But there would be even less honor involved in wedding one man whilst she was hopelessly in love with another.

Stiffly, she inched the betrothal ring from her finger.

"Oh, no," Justin protested. "You may still keep the ring."

Aurelia regarded the vulgar ruby in dismay. "I couldn't possibly. 'Tis a family heirloom. Your mother would never—"

"Oh, Mama wouldn't mind. Consider it a gesture of, er, friendship."

"No, please. You must take it back."

"Don't be a goose, Reely. 'Tis completely unnecessary."

"I insist!" Aurelia leaped up and seized his hand, slapping the ring into his open palm.

Justin shrugged cheerfully, pocketing the ring. "Oh, very well. If it will make you feel better . . ."

Aurelia sank back onto her chair's slick cushion. Nothing, she thought, would ever make her feel better. With what great ease the gentlemen in her life seemed able to dismiss her existence. Justin obviously experienced not so much as a pang of regret, and Everard would set sail today without once looking back. No! She had sworn she would not think about that.

Pressing her knuckles against her lips, Aurelia fought

back the sense of despair that had threatened to engulf her ever since her parting with Everard at Vauxhall. Surely he would come to see her one last time before—

"And we should have known years ago we would not suit," Justin was saying. "I expect that is why I have been dragging my heels over the wedding. You have turned into something out of the common way, a real beauty. But, dish me! When I kiss you, 'tis still like embracing my sister."

"I suppose that is because I am lacking in the art—" Aurelia stopped herself. Those were almost the same words she had spoken the night Everard had kissed her. Everard, who had made her feel she was *something out of the common way* long ago, when she well knew she was not.

An anxious note crept into Justin's otherwise complacent voice. "I hope you are not angry with me, are you Reely?"

"Angry? About what?" 'Twas she who was ending the engagement.

A hint of embarrassment spread across Justin's cheeks. "About what happened with Sylvie last night. 'Tis so unfair. I truly was innocent. I wish someone would believe me."

"It scarce matters. That is not the reason I decided to—"

"Oh, I know that. 'Tis because you have fallen in love with Everard."

Aurelia regarded Justin with an expression of horrified astonishment. For most of the time she had known Lord Spencer, he had always been blithely imperceptive, never guessing her secret feelings. Why did he have to begin now?

"Justin, I—I am so sorry," she stammered, unable to deny his words. "How did you—how could you possibly—"

"I'm not quite so thick-skulled as you might believe. You have done naught but sound out the man's virtues for

155

the past week. If I did not know Ramsey so well, I would swear from your description of him, he was a combination of Sir Galahad, Saint Peter, and—and Admiral Lord Nelson.''

Justin gingerly touched the ugly swelling along his cheekbone. "I have also had a few other hints as to how matters stand between you and Everard.''

"You mustn't put any of the blame upon him,'' Aurelia said quickly. "The fault is all mine. He doesn't even know about my decision to break the engagement. 'Tis none of it his doing.''

"Oh, no, indeed. I daresay I just imagined Everard planted me a facer last night. Mayhap I can even begin to imagine it doesn't still ache like the very devil.''

Aurelia could not have felt more stunned than if Justin had yanked the chair from beneath her. "Ev—Everard hit you?'' she gasped. She tried to picture the cool, imperturbable Everard so far gone in fury as to be capable of such a ruffianlike behavior—tried and failed.

"Why would Everard do a thing like that?''

Justin regarded her with a look of fond exasperation. "For the same reason knights were wont to charge off in defense of their fair damsels. I suppose I may consider myself lucky Ramsey doesn't own a lance.''

When she continued to stare at him uncomprehendingly, Justin chuckled, "The man's head over ears in love with you, you silly peagoose.''

"Oh, no—no, he couldn't possibly be.'' Aurelia shook her head, but was unable to quite still the sudden leaping of her heart. "He simply couldn't. Could he?'' she asked wistfully.

"Well, why else would he behave like such an idiot— knocking people down, preparing to fight a duel—'' Justin broke off, then groaned, "Oh, Lord!''

"A duel?'' Aurelia whispered, the word sending a trickle of ice along her spine.

Justin stood abruptly, then busied himself jabbing the poker into the empty fireplace grate, stirring long-dead coals. "Forget I said that. A jest, merely. In very poor taste."

But Aurelia stared at the broad expanse of his back, feeling as though her worst nightmares were about to come true. "You—you and Everard are going to fight a duel!"

"Good God, no!" Justin straightened, dropping the poker. "Ramsey is my closest friend and—and he isn't going to fight anyone—But if he were, it wouldn't be me."

With great difficulty, Aurelia restrained the urge to leap at Lord Spencer and throttle him. She managed to keep her voice calm, as though reasoning with an exasperating child.

"Then if this duel that is not going to be fought did take place, who *would* Everard's opponent be?"

"No one. No one at all, my dear." Justin flashed her his most disarming smile, but Aurelia shot to her feet. Fists clenched, she advanced on Lord Spencer.

"Justin, I swear if you do not tell me at once, I shall give your left cheek such a thump, it will match the other side."

"Damme, you're as mad as Ev." Justin retreated behind a backless Egyptian couch covered with embroidered silk. He stretched out one arm as though to ward her off. "Calm yourself, Reely, and sit down. I—I will tell you everything, though, the Lord knows, I shouldn't." He sighed. "The whole affair has been driving me nigh distracted, and that's the truth."

Although Aurelia scarce drew any comfort from his words, she forced herself to be seated upon the settee. Justin plunked down beside her, folding his arms across his chest.

"I am waiting," Aurelia said when he continued to be silent.

Looking as guilty as a small boy about to confess some

misdeed, Justin said, "Everard is set to meet Augustus Snape tomorrow morning."

"Snape!" Aurelia clutched Justin's sleeve.

"Aye." Justin nodded miserably. "The rogue made some rather insulting remarks about you. Ev should have let me pound the fellow into the ground, but instead he needs must challenge the little weasel. Gone completely off his head, Ev has.

"And Sylvie," Justin continued, "what must the spiteful wench do but put it into Snape's head to ask for pistols. Pistols!" Justin groaned, permitting his head to sag against his hands. "If it were swords, Ev could fight an entire regiment. But pistols! A blind man would have a better chance."

"Then the duel must be stopped." Aurelia was astonished her voice sounded so cool, when her emotions were in such a turmoil of fear and panic.

"Don't you think I haven't wracked my brains for a way to do so? But Ev completely refused to listen to me." Justin raked his fingers back through his sun-streaked hair. "He's supposed to be always getting me out of scrapes. 'Tis damnably disconcerting to have to be the sensible one."

He drooped his head dejectedly back against his hands. Aurelia ignored his obvious despair, her own lips hardening into a firm line of resolve.

"If Everard cannot be reasoned with, then we must use physical force to stop him. Even if you must render him senseless. We will kidnap him, force him to sail upon *The New Wind* as he'd planned."

Justin's eyes rounded in horror. "We cannot do anything like that, Reely. Why, Ev would never speak to me again. He has to go through with the duel. It's a question of honor."

"Honor!" Aurelia snapped. "Where is the honor in Everard's setting himself up like a wafer in a shooting gallery?"

"You don't understand, Reely, and there's no sense trying to make you."

"None whatsoever. I can see no good reason in the world for Everard to risk his life in this fashion. Why, I would not even put it beyond Augustus Snape to attempt to cheat."

"Impossible! I'm Ev's second. I would never permit any cheating. Besides," Justin added gloomily. " 'Tis completely unnecessary for Snape to do so. He's accredited to be a fair shot. I hope he will prove skilled enough to maim Ev and not accidently kill him."

But Aurelia found little consolation in such a hope. Choking back an unladylike oath, she rose briskly to her feet. 'Twas obvious Justin was not going to be of any help whatsoever. And she knew instinctively appealing to Everard would be to no avail. The devil take these men and their ridiculous notions of honor! Wouldn't she give Everard a blistering scold when this affair was over!

Over . . . A dreadful image rose before her eyes—Everard sprawled out upon the ground, the pristline lace of his cravat streaked bright red, Augustus Snape's sneer of triumph, his smoking pistol . . .

No! Aurelia shuddered. Not whilst there was breath left in her. No wretched toad like Snape was going to endanger the man she loved. With or without Justin's help, she would put a stop to this duel nonsense, no matter what she had to do. Aurelia clenched her hands into tight fists. *No matter what.*

Augustus Snape stared morosely at the evening shadows creeping up the plaster walls of his shabby lodgings, then poured himself another glass of gin. Blue Ruin, the local denizens of this down-at-the-heels part of London called the stuff, but the vile-tasting liquid could not prove more ruinous than last night's excitement at Vauxhall had been.

He raised the glass to his lips, wondering yet again if it would not be wiser to have bolted from London long before the sun rose tomorrow. Much as he had enjoyed the prospect of making mischief for Aurelia Sinclair, it had never been any part of his plan to risk his own precious hide. Plague take Everard Ramsey. Underneath those cool manners and unruffled gentlemanly appearance lurked a raving lunatic. Who would blame Augustus if he did not appear at Hyde Park tomorrow?

Everyone came the harsh answer. Snape took a huge gulp of the gin, grimacing as it burned his throat on the way down. Defaulting on a duel. Unforgivable offense, that. The story would be bound to leak out. He would lose forever what tenuous hold he had on the fringes of polite society and with it any chance of ever making a wealthy marriage.

Snape's bony hand slammed down against the wobbly pockmarked oak table. What a damned predicament. 'Twas that Fitzhurst bitch's doing. He should have rammed his fist down her throat. Prodding him along into accepting Ramsey's challenge! He should have known better than ever to get involved with the scheming creature. But when he'd seen an opportunity to punish Aurelia Sinclair for spurning him, the temptation had been irresistible. Damn it all, he was the third cousin to the Marquess of Scallingsforth, no matter what anyone thought. He had Miss Sinclair to thank for his present wretched circumstances. He could have been comfortably married by now. All that time he had wasted courting her, when he should have been scouting out another heiress. She had known all along she never intended to become Mrs. Augustus Snape, already had her sights upon being Lady Spencer. Well, he had vowed to make her rue the day, show her a thing or two about her precious Justin.

Draining his glass, Snape lolled his head against the top rail of the hard ladder-back chair. When had his plans begun to go awry? The scheme at Vauxhall had seemed simple enough. Lady Sylvie was to lure Lord Spencer off into the bushes, engage him in some compromising activity. Then Snape had but to maneuver Miss Sinclair into position so that she would have a good view of the proceedings. Exceedingly simple, but effective. How he had looked forward to savoring her humiliation when she caught her fiancé virtually flagrante delicto with Lady Sylvie.

But he had not counted upon Everard Ramsey's presence at the scene. Blast him! Snape scowled. There were some pretty smoky doings between Ramsey and Aurelia Sinclair. He was sure of it. Why else would the man go about slapping complete strangers, simply because they made chance remarks about the lady's virtue? In any event, Ramsey had completely put "paid" to his scheme for revenge. When Snape remembered that, he thought he would take great pleasure in putting a hole through the interfering jackanapes. If that was the way things turned out. Snape ran his finger nervously beneath his grime-ridden collar.

Lady Sylvie assured him that Ramsey was a notoriously bad shot. And although he had never crossed the sacred portals of White's himself, Snape had heard something of the jests about Ramsey's lack of skill with the pistols. Pouring himself another glass of gin, he kept reminding himself of those jests over and over again, trying to force his tensed muscles to relax.

But when a sharp rapping came against his door, he nearly shot through the cracks in the plaster ceiling. Feeling his heart thumping beneath his rib cage, he snarled, "Who is it? What the devil do you want?"

The door creaked open an inch, and his jowl-faced landlady thrust her nose into the room, each greasy coal-black hair upon her head seeming to bristle with indignation.

161

"Lady belowstairs," Mrs. Wiggins bit out. "Insists upon seeing you."

Lady? Snape rocked back in his chair. He knew of no woman, lady or otherwise, who would be tempted to call upon him in this district, just off Butcher's Row. Surely not even Lady Sylvie Fitzhurst— With a loud thud, Snape let the chair fall forward. He was about to tell Mrs. Wiggins to send the unknown female to perdition when curiosity got the better of his surly humor. Lurching to his feet, he strode out to the staircase landing to have a look at this creature bold or desperate enough to call upon a man at his lodgings. Mrs. Wiggins followed behind, her heavy jowls waggling with disapproval. "I run a respectable establishment here, Mr. Snape. If you be thinking of holding any sort of assignations under my roof, you can just think again."

Snape ignored her high, whining voice and studied the woman pacing the entryway below. Of medium height, her features were concealed by a heavy white veil, but along her back, he caught the gleam of one auburn curl. Snape's eyes narrowed, his tongue slithering across his lips.

"Ah, Mrs. Wiggins," Snape purred. " 'Tis a cousin of mine. She has come to bring me funds so that I can pay the arrears I am owing you."

Although Mrs. Wiggins sniffed with suspicion, greed won out over her sense of dubious propriety. She ambled down the steps to escort the lady above. As Aurelia Sinclair followed the plump landlady, she hugged her dove-gray skirts close against her, already regretting her reckless action in coming here. Only the thought of Everard's dark-fringed blue eyes closing in agony, kept her feet moving up the thread-bare carpeted treads.

Snape awaited her at the top of the stairs. "Good afternoon, my dear." With one white hand, he indicated the door to his apartment, a too-wide smile splitting his mouth.

Feeling very much like a harried fly winging near the web of a gangly-legged spider, Aurelia stepped inside.

Snape all but slammed the door in the face of his inquisitive landlady. Aurelia fingered her reticule, as she took in the sparsely furnished sitting room, the narrow alcove beyond which housed a rumpled four-poster bed. Studying the faded floral wallpaper and the holes gnawed in the wainscoting, Aurelia would not have been in the least surprised to feel rats whisking against the toes of her Roman sandals.

But then, she thought, as she forced herself to turn and face Snape, rats came in many forms and sizes. She would have preferred the kind that crept along the floor to the tall, slick-haired man who all but rubbed his hands together with glee.

"Well, well, well. Miss Sinclair. What an unexpected pleasure."

She started at his instant recognition, fought down the feelings of uneasiness and revulsion prickling along her skin as Snape stepped closer. With slow deliberation, she raised her veil, trying to steel her fingers from trembling. She had a part to play, and she must do it well. Everard's life depended upon it.

"Good afternoon, Mr. Snape," she said. "I trust I have not called at an inopportune moment." Her gaze shifted to the empty glass upon the table, and she crinkled her nose at the strong smell of spirits in the room. "If it were not the matter of utmost urgency, I should not—" She broke off with a gasp when Snape's clammy fingers closed round her own. Snatching her hand back before he could raise it to his moist lips, she struggled to keep the disgust from her eyes, all the while assuring herself that her maid and coach were just in the street outside. If Snape should so far forget himself as he did upon his last visit to Aldgate Manor, she could rush to the window and shout for her coachman.

Snape was naught but a cowardly bully. Indeed, 'twas his cowardice she was pinning all her hopes upon.

"Now, Miss Sinclair, you've no call to be nervous with me. I know some harsh words once passed between us. Let bygones be bygones, I always say."

"I entirely agree with you, sir." With great difficulty Aurelia mustered a smile. "Which is why I risked my reputation to come here to warn you."

Snape appeared more absorbed in groping for her hand than in paying heed to her words. Aurelia retreated a step closer to the window, but halted in her tracks when he chortled, "Why Miss Sinclair, whatever happened to your engagement ring?"

Flushing self-consciously, Aurelia whisked her hand behind her back. Trust Snape to notice a thing like that. His eyes glinted with malicious satisfaction. "Broke off the betrothal, did you, my dear? Cannot say as I blame you after Lord Spencer's behavior last night."

"I have not come here to discuss Lord Spencer."

"Ah, then perchance you have changed you mind about me, come to regard my attentions with more appreciation since you have discovered Lord Spencer's perfidy."

Aurelia shuddered, fearing she was going to be ill at the mere suggestion of such a thing. "No, sir. I have come here to save your life."

"My life?" Snape broke into cackling laughter. He strolled over to the table and poured himself another glass of gin. "And pray tell, Miss Sinclair, what inspires you to such tender solicitude upon my behalf?"

"I know all about the duel tomorrow. I had hoped to save you from Everard Ramsey."

"Save me? That's rich, upon my word. You appear to take a strong interest in that gentleman's doings, Miss Sinclair, what with taking him for guided tours of Vauxhall's dark walks and all. Mayhap 'twas not *you* who broke off the engagement."

Aurelia flushed, her lips tightening at Snape's insinuations, but she forced herself to remain calm. If she gave the odious man so much as a hint of her feelings for Everard, he would see through the fabric of lies she was about to weave. She affected a careless shrug, then lowered her veil as though about to leave.

"Alas, Mr. Snape, I did come, in all fairness, to warn you. But if you are not in the least particle interested to know what mortal danger—"

"Hah. Don't try any of that nonsense on me. I am quite familiar with Ramsey's reputation as a marksman. Why, they're giving five-to-one odds at White's that Ramsey will die as a result of the duel."

"Aye, that he will die, but those that place the wagers never mention how. But I quite see I am wasting my time talking with you. Regrettably, your mind is made up. Farewell, Mr. Snape."

Aurelia started for the door, but she had not gotten far when Snape caught her by the elbow. His eyes narrowed with suspicion, but his smirk had begun to waver.

"What do you mean—the wagers never mentioned how? How else would he die but by my shot?"

"There is always a hangman's noose." Aurelia firmly uncurled Snapes fingers from her sleeve.

"What are you talking about, you silly chit? Why, I know the law regarding dueling, but no one has ever actually received the death penalty."

Aurelia infused a mournful note into her voice. "Aye, but I fear, this time, Mr. Ramsey will have exhausted the good humor of the magistrates. Three men killed in less than two years. How will Everard—I mean Mr. Ramsey—ever explain away a fourth?"

She flung up her hands, affecting a started gasp. "Oh, dear, I should never have told you that. His poor family hushed up all the others, kept his dreadful secret for so long, even putting about the rumors of his poor marksmanship so that no one would believe—But I suppose I needn't worry." Grimacing beneath her veil, Aurelia forced herself to pat Snape's skeletal hand. "I daresay you will not be in a position to tell anyone after the morrow."

"What foolery is this?" Snape growled, but a fine mist of sweat began to bead upon his brow. "I know damned well Ramsey cannot shoot. I was told—"

"By whom, sir?"

"By Sylvie Fitzhurst." Aurelia could see some of Snape's confidence begin to fade with mere mention of the name.

"Lady Sylvie. I am sure the lady is well noted for her—her circumspection and keen judgement. The only testimony I have to offer you is the graves of three men who believed as you do."

Aurelia wrung her hands together in an imploring gesture, fearing she might be overdoing it, but a nervous tic had begun along Snape's jawline.

"I entreat you, Mr. Snape. If you have no regard for your own life, at least consider poor Mr. Ramsey's family. Even if he is not hung, this time he will surely be obliged to flee the country."

Snape swallowed, looking very much as though something were stuck in his gullet. He gave an uncertain laugh. "What—what a parcel of folderol. I don't believe a word of it. Now that you have lost Lord Spencer, you are obviously bent upon marrying Ramsey. That's why you want to stop the duel."

"Not in the least. I have no desire to live in France or be wed to such a madman. Who can say whom he will take it into his head to shoot next?"

Taking care to conceal her trembling fingers, Aurelia reached for the doorknob. "My conscience is now clear. I have never borne you any ill will, Mr. Snape. At least, I feel I have done my Christian duty by warning you."

She slowly opened the door, glad that Snape could not

see the perspiration trickling down her own cheeks beneath the veil. The man was looking decidedly shaken. When he raised his gin to his lips, the glass clinked against his teeth. She turned to fire one last parting shot. "I would be happy to do you one more favor, sir. Where does your mama live?"

"My mama?" Snape gaped at her. "In Cheapside. Why the deuce should you wish to—"

"I would be happy to call upon her"—Aurelia lowered her voice to a tender hush—"after . . . ."

The glass dropped from Snape's hand, shattering into a hundred pieces. With a gentle curtsy, Aurelia let herself out of the room. She scarce drew breath until her coachman was handing her into the safe confines of her own carriage.

Before the vehicle lumbered away, she stole one last glance up at the dirty panes that comprised Snape's window. Was he peering at her from behind the curtain even now, wondering, doubting? Had she played her part well enough? If only he had given her some definite sign that he was indeed terrified enough not to meet Everard on the morrow.

Aurelia bit down hard upon her lip. She had done her best, but she could not risk Everard's life on the mere chance that she had managed to frightened Snape away. No, she needed an alternative plan, something more direct. Something decidedly more desperate.

She shivered, her fingers tightening on her reticule as a dreadful notion popped into her head. No, she couldn't. Both Justin and Everard might hate her for it, but the more she considered the idea on the long ride back to Grosvenor Square, the more she became convinced there was no other way.

Chapter 10

The click of the surgeon's case being snapped open broke the early morning stillness of Hyde Park. Everard ground the toe of his boot into the dew-soaked grass and watched with an air of strange detachment as the portly, moon-faced doctor began to arrange his instruments in readiness. Justin, however, winced with the sight of every sharp blade the cheerful little man drew forth.

"Fine morning for your meeting, gentlemen," the doctor said, patting the ends of his bristly mustache. "I remember the dreadful rain when Lord Mifflin met Mr. Harbottle. Mr. Harbottle's blood soaked everywhere. O'course 'twas nothing compared to when Sir Norton challenged the Honorable Mr. Shaw. The sun was far too bright that day. Each shot the other, with Sir Norton's kneecap blown clear off. I thought I heard the bone crunch beneath my feet as I ran to him, but it turned out to be a piece of broken glass. Ha-Ha!"

Justin's features washed gray, nigh the same shade as the overcast sky. Everard gave his friend's shoulder a reassuring squeeze, at the same time wishing Snape would arrive so he could make an end to this affair. Slowly, he eased himself out of his double-breasted jacket of sapphire-blue superfine and tossed it carelessly to the ground.

Justin emitted a loud groan. "Blast it, Ev! I told you to wear something black, with small buttons."

Everard adjusted the hem of his red-and-white striped marcella waistcoat. He jutted one eyebrow upward with a faint trace of his customary self-mockery. "Black for morning wear, old fellow? The mere suggestion of such a thing is enough to chill my blood."

"But this is a duel, damn it. Not an—an al fresco breakfast." Justin raked his hand back through his hair, a gesture he had indulged in repeatedly since arising. "And that starched cravat. You might as well have painted a bull's-eye upon yourself and be done with it."

"I have arranged my cravat to perfection every morning since I can remember. 'Tis the one thing I do well." Everard's mouth crooked into a wry half smile. "You would hardly expect me to leave off now."

"I would expect—oh, what the devil's the use in talking to you?" Justin tore at his hair again. The ends were beginning to bristle up in such a fashion as made him appear as if he had just crawled from his bed. Everard would have found the effect amusing, but for the anxiety and fear he saw mirrored in his friend's eyes. 'Twas curiously touching to see the carefree Justin so troubled upon his behalf. He shook Justin's hand in a firm clasp.

"Justin, in case I have neglected to tell you, I am dashed grateful for—"

But Justin jerked away from him. "No! No, blister it! Don't talk as if you were going to . . . You will dispatch that varlet Snape, and we will soon be making merry at breakfast. I firmly believe that."

And some otherwise sensible folk believe in the second coming of King Arthur, Everard thought, but did not voice it. Justin was looking miserable enough. As for himself, he felt nothing at the imminent prospect of the duel, only a kind of emptiness. He reviewed mentally all the preparations he had made, attempting to determine whether he had forgotten anything. He'd left instructions with his solicitor regarding his will, a letter to be delivered to his parents, in case Snape's aim proved too accurate. And a message for Aurelia as well.

With her image shimmering in his mind, some of Everard's feelings of impassivity began to waver. How he had longed to see her one last time, hold her, tell her . . . No, even faced with the prospect of his own death, there was nothing he could tell her, nothing that he had the right to say. It had taken the better part of the night for him to compose a simple farewell letter. In the end he could pen naught but a single line, "God bless you, my dearest friend—and keep you."

Justin jostled against Everard as he drew forth his pocket watch. "Snape is late. I told you he was no gentleman. I think we should leave and forget—"

"Your timepiece is too fast. In any event, I believe that is my worthy opponent arriving now." Everard indicated an open-topped carriage rumbling through the gates of the park's brick enclosure. But as the coach drew nearer, the only discernible passengers were a heavily-veiled woman accompanied by her maid.

"I would wager there goes a lady of most passionate disposition," Everard remarked in languid tones after the carriage had rumbled past, disappearing behind a line of trees. " 'Tis passing early to be abroad on an amorous adventure."

"It wouldn't surprise me if it were Sylvie," Justin said. "She is vindictive enough to enjoy watching you—" He swallowed, allowing the grim thought to remain incomplete.

"Well, your mistress did go to great lengths to arrange this entertainment. I trust she will not be disappointed."

"Harpy! She's no mistress of mine. I'll have no more to do with the wench."

"I am glad to hear that," Everard said softly. "Especially for Aurelia's sake."

"I don't know how much it would matter to Reely. Now that the engagement is off." Justin turned his gaze back to the doctor. He crinkled his nose in distaste. "Plague take it. That fellow's brought enough of those gruesome instruments with him to operate on half of Wellington's army."

But Everard scarce heeded the last part of Justin's speech. His hand clamped around Justin's wrist in a vise-like grip. "What did you say?"

"I said that fellow has enough blades to—"

"No, I mean about the engagement."

"Oh, didn't I tell you?" Justin said, his manner a trifle too casual. "Reely's called it off."

"Called it off? Damn you, Justin! How could you let that happen. Didn't you apologize to her for what happened last night?"

Justin managed to free himself from Everard's bone-crushing grip. Grimacing, he rubbed his wrist. "Well, I tried, but she didn't care about me and Sylvie. That's not the reason she doesn't want to marry me. She—" He broke off, giving Everard a wary look. "She'd have my head if I told you the real reason, and between the pair of you, I don't know which is the more dangerous. I had hoped that after this was over . . ."

"You had hoped what?" Everard asked sharply. His one consolation in going through with this affair with Snape had been the knowledge that although Aurelia might grieve a little for him, she would soon be safely wed to Justin.

Justin shuffled his feet. "Reely made me promise I would not tell you, but, oh, hang it all! You've a right to know before you face Snape. She's fallen in love with you, Ev."

"That's nonsense! 'Tis you she loves—has loved all her life."

171

"As a brother, perhaps." Justin shrugged. "I did try to tell you there was nothing romantic between us."

Everard opened his mouth to protest, then closed it again. He could scarce credit what Justin was telling him. It was such a dangerous hope. Already his heart was soaring with it; he was beginning to imagine all sorts of impossible things.

He compressed his lips sternly. "Justin, if you are feeding me another of your Banbury tales . . ."

"Upon my honor, 'tis true. Reely told me so herself. Do you think I would tell you such a thing in jest?"

Everard slowly shook his head. "No, but I can still scarce believe it. Why—why would she . . ."

"Prefer you to me?" For the first time that morning, Justin grinned. "Hanged if I know. I think it has something to do with the way you tie your cravats."

Everard gave a shaky chuckle. Aurelia free of her engagement and possibly in love with him? Was he dreaming? Of a sudden, he had difficulty meeting Justin's eye. "I—I suppose you have guessed my feelings for her. I never meant it to happen, to betray our friendship in this manner."

"Don't be such a clunch, Ev. Why, I couldn't be happier if you had fallen in love with my own sister. In fact. I wouldn't have wished Clarice upon my worst enemy. The only betrayal I will feel is if you don't ask me to stand up with you at the wedding."

Wedding? It occurred to Everard that Justin was speaking of *his* wedding—his wedding to Aurelia. He tipped back his head, staring at the dull gray clouds scudding by. Never had the English skies appeared so blue to him, the sun so brilliant. Laughter rumbled deep in his chest, which Justin's voice echoed. Justin dealt him a playful buffet on the shoulder, which he returned, all the while trading quips about finally losing one's heart and slipping one's neck into the matrimonial noose. Everard felt almost drunk with the joy flooding through him.

The sound of curricle wheels upon the gravel path doused his high spirits like a cold-water bath. He glanced around, his smile freezing upon his lips at the same time he saw Justin's grin fade.

Augustus Snape had finally arrived.

From her place of concealment behind the broad-based trunk of an oak tree, Aurelia stared through the haze of her veil at Justin and Everard. Her stomach tensed until she thought she was going to be ill when she saw the surgeon preparing his scalpel. As Everard and Justin began laughing, playfully slapping each other on the back, Aurelia thought she could have gladly shot them both herself. How could they be romping like a pair of schoolboys out on a lark, when Everard might soon be fighting for his life? She was relieved when they both became more somber, relieved until she noted what had put an end to their mirth.

Like a tall, thin shadow creeping across the grass, Augustus Snape marched toward Everard. Aurelia pressed her hand against her breast, feeling iron bands of fear tighten about her heart. Her scheme had not worked. Snape had not believed her. Frantically she glanced toward the park's iron gates. But it was obvious no other source of help was coming. She was forced to revert to her final, most desperate plan. Her hand inched inside the voluminous pocket of her drab brown cloak weighted down by the pistol. She eased her sweating palm around the smooth wooden handle. The weapon was primed and ready. Had she loaded it correctly? She prayed she had, prayed she wouldn't actually be forced to use it.

She stepped out of her place of concealment and began walking slowly toward the group of men, who were as yet unaware of her presence. Her heart thudded with every

173

step. She expected at any moment to see Everard distance himself from Snape, their seconds handing them the weapons.

Their seconds . . . Aurelia halted in midstep. But Snape had arrived alone. She was not completely clear on the codes of dueling, but she was certain both combatants were required to have a second present. Otherwise, the meeting could not take place, could it? Renewed hope began to flicker inside of her. She waited. Yes, something of a peculiar nature definitely was taking place.

Aurelia eased her grip on the pistol. Even from this distance, it was not difficult to see that Snape was fawning over Everard, rubbing his bony hands together, cringing in an almost servile manner. 'Twas almost as if Snape were . . .

"Apologizing." Aurelia breathed, but she dared not feel any sensation of relief, for Everard stood rigid, staring at Snape's outstretched hand.

Please, Everard, I beg you, Aurelia silently prayed. Accept his apology. Accept it.

The minutes seemed to stretch into hours. Her gaze never wavered from Everard's unruly dark hair, the unyielding cast of his aquiline profile. With that uncanny sense of his, he suddenly turned and stared straight in her direction, as though she had called his name aloud.

Then slowly he favored Snape with a curt nod and touched his hand in reluctant acknowledgement.

"Thank God!" Aurelia choked on a half sob. All the tension, the fear, rushing out of her system left her feeling nigh giddy, but she managed to keep her knees from buckling beneath her. Even from this distance, she could sense Everard's eyes upon her, the softening of his expression, the slight tremor of his sensitive mouth as it tipped into his half smile.

She drew in a tremulous breath, her pulse quickening as Everard started toward her across the lawn. For a brief moment she saw nothing but him. Then the pounding of horse's hooves penetrated her consciousness. She shifted her gaze long enough to note a burly constable dismounting. He and two other officials bore purposefully down upon Everard and Justin.

"Oh, no!" Aurelia moaned in dismay. "Not now, you silly fools."

She started to race forward, to tell the officers to go away, their intervention was unnecessary. But 'twas already too late to halt what she had set in motion the evening before.

The beaming constable had seized an astonished Everard by the arm. "In the King's name, I command you gents to set aside your weapons and come peacefully with me. You are all under arrest."

Seated across from Lady Foxcliff in the cozy little parlor at the back of her ladyship's town house, Aurelia slumped down on the divan. Dolefully she finished her tale of how she had broken her engagement with Justin and then taken steps to put a stop to the duel.

" . . . and then when I wasn't sure if I had frightened Snape away, I laid information against Everard with the magistrate. I tried to tell the constable I was mistaken about the duel, but what with the surgeon being there and and the pistol case, he wouldn't listen. Both Everard and Justin have—have been taken away."

Aurelia waited, certain that her ladyship would look justifiably vexed to hear that her favorite nephew had been arrested. Instead, Lady Foxcliff flung back her head and guffawed so hard, she appeared likely to fall off the thin-legged Chippendale chair upon which she perched.

"Lord, 'tis better than a farce at Drury Lane. Serves him right. What was the boy thinking of to be dueling in Hyde Park! I would give a monkey to have seen Ramsey's face when that beef-witted constable hustled him off."

"Neither he nor Justin looked too pleased with me." Aurelia sighed. "Though I don't think Everard was quite so angry until the pistol in my pocket went off and nearly shot him in the foot."

Lady Foxcliff stomped her foot and clutched her sides, tears of mirth streaming from her eyes. Her ladyship's laughter was infectious. Despite herself, Aurelia's lips curved into a reluctant smile, although she complained, "It did seem quite unfair of Everard. He was most eager to stand up and deliberately let Augustus Snape try to wound him, but when I almost did the same by accident, he was furious."

Her ladyship swiped at her moist eyes. Her chuckles abated long enough for her to deal Aurelia a hearty reassuring smack on the shoulder. "Now, my dear, don't fret yourself. I know how these affairs go. The magistrate will wink one eye and deliver some long-winded homily on the evils of dueling. Ramsey will be back here to plague you before the cat can lick its whiskers, so you run along upstairs and put on your prettiest frock and settle down to wait for the scamp."

Aurelia opened her mouth to protest, then blushed under the knowing look her ladyship was giving her. Much reassured by Lady Foxcliff's attitude toward the disconcerting turn of events, Aurelia whisked upstairs to her room to obey. It took her the better part of an hour to select a gown, dismissing first this one and then that, until she nigh drove her maid to distraction. Finally she settled upon a day dress of dark green satin with goblet-shaped cuffs, embroidered at the hem in a geometric pattern of pale pink.

But the morning stretched into late afternoon with no sign of Everard. By the time tea was laid out in the parlor, Aurelia had rearranged the delicate Sevres cups and silver spoons upon the mahogany serving table at least a dozen times. Her ladyship's cook had served up a platter of the most delectable strawberry tarts. Although Aurelia's stomach was knotted with tension, she felt the old desire to ease her nervous pangs by gobbling up every last one. She inched the plate closer, then resolutely shoved it aside. No, Everard would be excessively disappointed if he found her giving way to temptation. Who knew what havoc she might have already wreaked upon her figure since coming to London?

Anxiously she hurried over to study herself in one of the pier glasses set between the tall windows which opened out into the gardens. For once, she set aside her habit of self-criticism and tried to see herself as Everard would when he walked in the room.

There was a soft glow in her eyes she'd never seen before, and the glossy auburn curls framing her face enhanced the creaminess of her skin. Perhaps it was all owing to the elegance of the gown, which made her look supple and slender.

She raised one hand, tentatively touching her flushed cheek. "I—I am almost beautiful, am I not, Everard?" she whispered. Mayhap it was not so absurd to think that he could be in love with her, as Justin insisted. She thought back to all the time he had spent with her last winter. Why else would he have taken such pains with her, scolding, encouraging, setting aside all his customary pursuits? She had been a fool not to realize it before. Everard *did* love her.

She stood a little taller, confidence fluttering to life inside her like a butterfly testing its wings for the first time. Her heart began to thud with anticipation when she heard a footfall upon the carpeted hallway outside the door. With a slight spring in her step, she sat back down by the tea tray, gracefully arranging her skirts, and settled her hands primly upon her lap.

Her ladyship's surly butler stepped inside long enough to announce, "Lady Sylvie Fitzhurst."

Before Aurelia had time to protest, Lady Sylvie swept

into the room and the butler closed the door behind her. Aurelia stared at the woman with less than cordiality. Lady Sylvie's eyes were darting daggers back at her, despite the feline smile fixed upon her ladyship's face.

"Good afternoon, Miss Sinclair."

Aurelia rose to her feet with slow dignity. "You astonish me, Lady Sylvie. I would not have thought that even you would be bold enough to come where you must assuredly know you will not be welcome."

Aurelia was astonished by the chilling accents of her voice. If only her mother could have heard her. Lady Sylvie flinched, but she stepped further into the room. An angry titter escaped her.

"I daresay you are wroth with me over what happened at Vauxhall. I—"

"Not in the least. I never overly concern myself with such *trivial* matters."

"But you and Lord Spencer are still engaged?"

"Is that what you have come here to discover?" Aurelia arched one eyebrow mockingly, while feeling an inner sense of triumph. She had learned more than she realized from Everard this past winter. She only regretted she did not have a quizzing glass. "I should hate for you to perish from curiosity. We have indeed broken off the betrothal."

Lady Sylvie's smile widened, only to vanish as Aurelia continued, "But it had naught to do with you. Heavens! If one became angry every time Justin decided to kiss another pretty wench, er, I mean lady . . ." Aurelia indulged in a silvery laugh. "Not that this information will be of any use to you, my dear Lady Sylvie. I doubt your charms will be enough to tempt Justin again, especially considering you did your best to endanger the life of his closest friend."

Aurelia permitted her gaze to rove over Lady Sylvie's frame in disparaging fashion. The woman's ample bosom quivered with suppressed fury, an unbecoming red mottling her cheeks. Aurelia was half tempted to examine her own hands to see if she had sprouted velvet claws. Never in her life had she treated another woman in such cutting fashion, but then, never had one so threatened the man she loved. She half expected Lady Sylvie to hiss like a furious serpent, then storm out of the room.

But with great visible effort, Lady Sylvie checked herself. She sat down upon the divan, and began to pour out a cup of tea.

Aurelia gently removed the cup and saucer from her grasp. "You won't have time for that. You're leaving now."

Lady Sylvie's eyes spit venom. "I talked with Augustus Snape earlier and heard how you frightened him off from the duel. I suppose you are feeling rather clever at the moment."

"Yes," Aurelia agreed affably. "I did think it was rather a brilliant stroke upon my part.".

Sylvie sniffed. "One wonders how such a *clever* woman can permit a man like Everard Ramsey to make a fool of her." She picked up a butter knife and began to tool it between her fingers. "For you will look a fool, Miss Sinclair, when the story of Ramsey's infamous wager leaks out."

Aurelia feigned a yawn. "Mr. Ramsey has a penchant for involving himself in so many wagers. I can scarce be expected to keep track of them all. To which one are you referring?"

"The one where he wagered he could turn some poor dowdy creature into this season's belle. How fortunate you must feel that he chose you. But, of course, it never does a lady's reputation any good to be the vulgar object of a bet."

"W-what are you talking about?" Aurelia felt some of her confidence begin to waver, but she shook off the sinking feeling. She would be a dolt to believe anything Sylvie Fitzhurst had to say. 'Twas obvious the woman, having been balked in the matter of the duel, was seeking some new form of spite.

Lady Sylvie's eyes narrowed. She gave a throaty laugh. "Why, my dear, can it be you did not know? Everard Ramsey made a wager with his aunt that he could turn even you into a beauty. Of course, to my mind, the degree of his success is questionable, but I have heard that Lady Foxcliff was satisfied enough to concede the bet."

"Neither Lady Foxcliff nor Everard—" Aurelia began, then halted, her mouth suddenly going dry. An unwelcome memory surfaced in her mind of her first night in London as she had nervously prepared for the Carlisle ball, then presented herself in the drawing room for Everard's inspection. Her ladyship had laughingly remarked, *"Stap me, Ev. You must take the money. Never was a wager so fairly won."* Everard had promptly shushed his aunt. Aurelia had been too anxious for some sign of Everard's approval to question the strange comment then. But now . . .

She gripped the back of the divan, wanting to refute Lady Sylvie's hateful words, wanting to, but unable. Why did it make so much more sense, why was it easier to believe that Everard's attentions were the result of a wager than his being in love with her? How had she ever dared to fancy such a thing? Herself beautiful, desirable. Bah!

She felt as though Lady Sylvie dealt her a blow to the stomach instead of an insidiously soft pat upon the hand. "Perhaps you should sit down, Miss Sinclair. You don't look at all well."

Aurelia wrenched her hand away, a sharp driving sense of anger suddenly taking possession of her, leaving her shaking from head to toe. How dare Everard Ramsey! *How dare he* sweep into her world, make such unsettling changes in her existence, and all for a wager, for sport, for his own amusement. She'd been perfectly content as she was in the old days. If not content, at least she had still had her pride, her sense of humor. The knowledge of this stupid wager somehow robbed her of both in one fell stroke. Tears of fury burned in her eyes; her hands were clenched into tight fists until her nails nigh drew blood from her palms.

'Twas at this unfortunate moment that Everard Ramsey strode down the hallway to the parlor. Feeling more nervous than he could ever remember, he paused just outside the door, patting his waistcoat to make certain the ring was still safe. He was determined to make a better job of his proposal than he had seen Justin do.

"Your guardian angel, Ev," Justin had laughingly referred to Aurelia, and he was right. 'Twas certain that she had had something to do with Snape's withdrawal from the duel, though how she had accomplished it, Everard couldn't begin to guess.

His mouth tilted into a soft smile. To perdition with all the fancy phrases he had been rehearsing. His heart was too full for that. He would sweep her into his arms immediately and be done with it. Turning the knob, he stepped quietly into the room.

Aurelia had her back to him, her auburn curls tumbling in charming disarray along the graceful curve of her neck. He noted with great tenderness that she was trembling.

"Aurelia." He breathed her name, covering the distance between them in two quick strides. Slowly, she turned.

His arms closed about her before she looked up at him, bracing the heels of her hands against his chest. As he bent to kiss her, it occurred to Everard, his angel appeared to have twin devils burning in her vivid green eyes.

He hesitated, repeating more uncertainly this time, "Aurelia?"

"Is it true?" she asked tersely.

"Is—is what true?" Everard sensed some impending disaster about to overtake him, but had not the least notion what. Was she still upset over something involving the duel?

181

"Is it true that there was a wager between you and your aunt as to whether you could turn me into a beauty?"

The guilty flush spreading across Everard's cheeks condemned him before he could even reply, "Well, yes, but—"

He never had opportunity to finish. She drew back her arm and cracked him with the full force of her open palm across the jaw. Everard staggered back in astonishment, raising his hand to rub his stinging cheek. What the deuce? Then he noticed they were not alone in the room. Lady Sylvie Fitzhurst had retreated to the window seat and stood watching, a malicious smirk upon her face, as though waiting for the curtain to ring up upon some choice bit of entertainment.

It took no great stretch of the imagination for Everard to guess what had happened. That night at Vauxhall, Lady Sylvie must have overheard his aunt's unfortunate remarks about the wager. But God knows how devilishly the woman had twisted the facts when repeating the tale to Aurelia. Everard straightened. Well, he had no intentions of putting on a performance to satisfy Sylvie Fitzhurst's warped sense of malice. He would settle this with Aurelia privately.

"Aurelia, my dear," he began patiently. "If you will strive to compose yourself, we can—"

"I don't want to compose myself. Tell me, Mr. Ramsey, how much did you win? I should like to know exactly how much I was worth to you."

"Stop it, Aurelia." He spoke more sternly this time, trying to capture her hands. She whipped away from him with an expression of revulsion that hurt him more than the slap had done.

She gave a bitter, strangled laugh. "I suppose to a gentleman with your penchant for gaming, the whole thing was trivial, just another lark, but I trust you won enough to have made it worth your while. You were put to such pains to achieve your effect."

182

Everard froze, his hand half-extended toward her in a gesture of appeal. It would not have surprised him for his father or anyone else to believe him capable of conducting such a heartless wager, but for Aurelia to do so and on the mere word of a viper like Sylvie Fitzhurst! He lowered his outstretched hand slowly back to his side.

Aurelia was too far gone in her own misery to note the flash of pain in Everard's eyes before he hooded their expression. If only he would deny he had done this dreadful, hurtful thing, instead of standing there looking so cold, so remote.

"I—I am waiting for your explanation," she said.

He hunched his shoulders. "What explanation is necessary? Lady Sylvie appears to have already told you everything you need to know."

His casual dismissal of her pain cut Aurelia worse than the fact of the wager itself. He was not even going to attempt to apologize. She fought back the tears that threatened to spill down her cheeks at any moment.

"Oh, how I despise you." She choked. "I—I wish I had never met you. I wish I had shot you myself. I— I . . ."

"There is no need for you to elaborate further." Everard interrupted, his eyes flintlike, his features appearing carved from stone. "You have made your feelings abundantly clear."

Turning on his heel, he strode from the room, slamming the door behind him. Aurelia's shoulders began to shake. She sank down upon the divan, pummeling the bolster as tears of impotent rage spilled down her face, rage at herself as much as Everard. How could she have been foolish enough to think she had fallen in love with such a cold-hearted man?

She completely forgot Lady Sylvie's presence in the room, until the woman clapped her hands together, calling out mockingly, "Bravo, Miss Sinclair."

Aurelia swiped the moisture from her cheeks as her ladyship glided over to her. She clung desperately to her anger, for she knew when it was gone, the pain would begin. She could feel the dulling edges of it tugging at her heart already.

"There, there, my dear," Lady Sylvie cooed. "Forget the worthless man and enjoy your tea."

With a sneer upon her lips, she handed Aurelia a china plate bearing a large strawberry tart. Aurelia sniffed, staring at the succulent pastry, feeling she had come full circle. Once again, the only consolation in her life seemed to be food. And what did it matter to anyone what she looked like? Certainly not to Everard Ramsey.

Aurelia's fingers clamped around the plate. Damn Everard Ramsey! It did matter. It mattered to someone very important. It mattered to Aurelia Sinclair.

"Go ahead, my dear," Lady Sylvie prodded. "After what you have been through, you deserve to indulge yourself a little."

Aurelia drew in a shuddering breath, then stared up at her ladyship. "You're absolutely right. I do."

No, Aurelia! She could almost hear her mother's voice. *A lady would never—* But for the first time in her life, Aurelia gave little credence to her mother's dictums.

She scooped up the delicate pastry and crammed it against Lady Sylvie's face. The woman tried to gasp, but was choked by the crumbs and flowing red berries dripping down her chin into the neckline of her low-cut bodice.

As Aurelia stalked out of the room, she could still hear Lady Sylvie's muffled shrieks.

Chapter 11

Justin watched with an expression of baffled dismay as the last of Aurelia's portmanteau was slung on the back of the chaise-and-four.

"But—but Reely, you cannot be set upon leaving this way, not even giving Ev a chance to explain."

"When I last saw Mr. Ramsey, he evinced no desire to explain anything," Aurelia said in taut accents. Nearly a week had passed since her quarrel with Everard. For all she knew or *cared*, she thought fiercely, he might have sailed off the end of the world. She glanced around the stable yard, pretending to ascertain whether Wallis had forgotten to hand up her smallest dressing case, in reality taking a moment to conceal the tears swimming in her eyes.

"Well, blast it all, you did tell the man you never wanted to see him again."

But he didn't have to be so quick to believe me, Aurelia thought, but she halted the forlorn slump of her shoulders. She said briskly, "Lady Foxcliff has promised to send on the rest of my things later. So I believe that takes care of everything."

Justin scowled. "No, it doesn't. Not by a long shot, and you know it."

"Did Everard send you here to act as his emissary?"

Despite herself, Aurelia could not suppress the hopeful quiver in her voice.

"No, but—"

She sighed, then thrust out her hand. "Then let us part friends, Justin and say no more about it before we end by quarreling, too."

Reluctantly he took her hand. "But, Reely, all I wanted to say was—"

"It should be lovely in Norfolk this time of year." She spoke up, deliberately interrupting him. "I shall call upon your sister and write you a full report on how your new nephew is doing."

"Aurelia!" Justin's fingers crushed down around hers. "Hang it all, will you please listen to me for but five minutes?"

She shook her head. "No, Justin, please. I—I have had Lady Foxcliff haranguing me all morning."

"Then she must have explained to you about the wager."

"She did, but it makes no difference."

Justin gaped at her in bewilderment as Aurelia struggled to put into words what she did not quite understand herself, the feeling that she was as much to blame for the quarrel as Everard. Her old self-doubts had gotten the better of her, making her incapable of believing that she was worthy of being loved. Even if she could change that, 'twas too late. She knew she had said some things to Everard that were unforgivable.

"There—there are some fences that cannot be mended," she said, swallowing back her tears. "Now, please Justin, just bid me farewell."

Justin looked more as though he would have liked to shake her, but instead he bent down and lightly brushed his lips against her cheek. After he had seen Aurelia and her maid bestowed safely in the coach, he could not resist one final appeal.

"But, Reely, Ev doesn't even know that you are going away. What shall I tell him?"

"Tell him"—she sighed wearily—"tell him anything that you like."

The coachman whipped up the team and the chaise rumbled out of the stable yard. Scowling, Justin stood staring long after it had vanished from sight. If this wasn't the damnedest situation! When two of the most sensible people he knew could behave in such absurd, mule-headed fashion, why, they might as well unlock the doors of Bedlam and let all the lunatics loose.

Justin raked his fingers back through his hair. He would soon be bald at this rate. 'Twas a novel experience for him, this business of becoming so deeply involved in other people's problems. Uncomfortable and exasperating! He wanted simply to forget the whole thing. Leave Ev and Reely to sort it out on their own. But neither of them seemed capable of doing so.

Damn! He'd never have any peace until this was settled. But now with Reely haring off back to Aldgate, what was he going to say to Ev? Nothing would induce Ramsey to go after her. The fellow was like to choke on his pride.

"Tell him anything you like," Reely had said. Hah! Tell him anything . . . Justin blinked, as the glimmer of an idea came to him. But no, he couldn't tell Ev a thing like that. Why, Reely would flay him alive.

The corners of Justin's mouth upturned in a grin of pure mischief. Ah, but what reproach could she make? She *had* given him permission.

Everard's dapper little valet wrung his hands, tears all but springing to his eyes as he watched his master don his new suit of clothes.

"Oh, sir, that I should live to see this day!" Beddoes moaned.

Ignoring the man's wails, Everard faced himself in the

cheval glass. He deftly tied his cravat in a plain style to match the severe cut of his navy jacket of fustian and the unremarkable somberness of his waistcoat and breeches.

Beddoes sniffed. "If you have no regard for your own reputation sir, then think of mine."

Despite his gloomy frame of mind, which quite matched the apparel, a reluctant smile tugged at Everard's lips. "Do not distress yourself unduly. I shall make it clear to all and sundry you had no part in this."

"But why, sir? Why are you doing this? You, the most elegant gentleman in England, saving only Mr. Brummell."

"It is high time I earned a reputation for something besides being a frivolous coxcomb and the way I cut a deck of cards." His mouth set into a hard line, Everard turned back to face his reflection in the mirror. Then, Miss Sinclair, he thought, perhaps you will have a higher opinion of me than to believe . . .

Suppressing the rest of the notion, he attacked his unruly mane of dark hair with a comb, attempting to whip it in line with his new, more sober image. 'Twas a hopeless task, but at least it gave him something to concentrate his energies upon. His emotions had run the gamut this past week, bitterness, anger at Aurelia, despair. He had almost responded to her doubts the same way he always had to his father's. By indulging in a wild round of gaming to show her how right she was. But something held him back. He was growing too old for such boy's tricks.

He would shed his ne'er-do-well image if it killed him. Hadn't Aurelia once told him he could do anything he put his mind to? Well, he would prove to her how serious-minded he could be. And then . . . A gleam of gold on the dressing table caught his eye. He slipped the engagement ring he had bought Aurelia inside his waistcoat pocket. It would stay there, he resolved, until the day she would be proud to wear it upon her finger. He began to brush down his lapels, trying not to grimace at the sight of the dully clad figure the mirror reflected back, when a loud banging sounded on the door to his lodgings.

Dispatching Beddoes to get rid of the impertinent caller who came bothering him at this hour of the morning, Everard fought down the urge to reach for his quizzing glass and attach it round his neck.

The door slammed. He heard Beddoes's muffled cry as Justin shoved his way into the room.

"Ev, thank God I've found you in."

Everard turned slowly to face his friend. It occurred to him that Justin was looking more distressed than he had the morning of the duel. His hair practically stood on end, but he halted in midstride, looking considerably taken aback as he studied Everard from crown to toe.

"Stap me, Ev! Who has died?"

"No one." Everard's lips tightened in annoyance. "What the deuce do you mean by bursting in here like—"

Justin seemed to snap to attention as though remembering the purpose of his errand. "It's Reely, Ev. She . . ." He trailed off, glancing significantly in Beddoes's direction.

The valet sniffed. "If you will excuse me, sir. I shall go see about procuring more champagne for the boot blacking. I trust we are still going to keep our boots polished?"

At Everard's frowning nod, the small man favored Justin with a dignified bow before quitting the room.

"Now what is this nonsense about Aurelia?"

"She's run off, Ev. Left your aunt's house this morning."

Everard steeled his features to remain impassive. "She most likely had decided to return to Aldgate. 'Twas always her intention."

"No! She has gone off with Snape!"

"What!" Everard arched one eyebrow, regarding Justin

189

as though he had taken leave of his senses. His friend paced about the room with all the grace of an agitated bear.

" 'Tis true. They are going to be married. You must go after her before 'tis too late.''

But Everard crossed his arms over his chest. "Now where did you get such a humbug tale as that? Why would Aurelia ever consider wedding Augustus Snape?'' he asked sharply. Sometimes Justin's jests went beyond the bounds of good taste. But there was an earnest look in his friend's eye that began to make Everard feel uneasy.

"Because she promised him, that's why.'' Justin stopped his pacing. "The woman's so mad with love for you, she'd do anything.''

"I fail to follow the logic of that. If Aurelia is so much in love with me as you say—''

"Blister me! When was there anything logical where women are concerned?'' Justin seized Everard by the shoulders. "I tell you, we don't have time to stand here talking, you great dolt. We both wondered why Snape suddenly decided to apologize and call off the duel. Well, I feared when Reely left me that day, she was going to do something desperate to save you. She promised to marry that sniveling fortune hunter.''

Everard slowly uncrossed his arms. "But—but how did you discover all this?''

"She left me a note, but her maid delivered it too soon. Reely begged me to try to make you understand. That was why she quarreled with you that day.'' Justin sighed, staring down at the carpet. "She thought if you hated her, it would make matters easier.''

Everard felt the color draining from his face. "Easier!'' he said chokingly. "To see her the wife of that miscreant! I'll see Snape in hell first!''

Striding to the door, Everard bellowed for his valet, then tore about the room in search of his boots. Aurelia and Snape! The mere thought was enough to make his flesh crawl. As he began ramming on his boots, he commanded Justin, "Give me her letter. She must have left some clue as to their destination."

"Er, no! She didn't! I—I mean in my haste to find you, I forgot the note. But I believe they are going to Aldgate."

"Aldgate?" Everard checked in the act of putting on his boot to stare up at Justin.

"You cannot think Reely would ever stand for being wed over the anvil at Gretna Green. No, I am almost positive her letter said something about a special license."

"A special license! Then they could well be married before I . . ." Everard left the horrible thought unfinished. It didn't matter, he told himself grimly. Even if she was wed, Aurelia would be a widow before the sun set tonight. Not waiting for Beddoes, he flung some of his belongings haphazardly into a valise.

"I shall have to hire a vehicle," he groaned. How much precious time had he lost already?

"No, you take my phaeton and head toward Aldgate," Justin said, firmly steering him toward the door. "I'll obtain another coach and follow the North Road, just in case I have guessed wrong."

Everard nodded in grim agreement. When Justin saw the frantic light glittering in Ramsey's blue eyes, he almost relented. And when he saw the reckless fashion in which Everard whipped up his team of horses and tore down the narrow cobblestone street, Justin experienced more than a small twinge of conscience.

Mayhap he had gone too far this time in playing one of his little jests. For a full minute, he worried about the consequences of what he had done. Then he shrugged. What could possibly go wrong? Ev would overtake Reely on the road. They would fall into each other's arms, and all misunderstandings would be cleared away. They would both thank him for this later. Justin drew in a deep breath. It was a fine spring morning, promising to be a beautiful day.

Mayhap he should call upon the voluptuous Lady Carlisle and see if she would care for a drive in the park. Whistling cheerfully, Lord Spencer strolled off down St. James Street.

The baby's squalls only increased in volume as Lady Norton proudly handed her offspring into the vicar's out-stretched arms. Aurelia shifted wearily from foot to foot, her eyes wandering past the small gathering of friends and neighbors as she gazed about the light, airy interior of Ald-gate's tiny church. Then she caught herself and focused her attention back upon the babe, trying to look deeply interested in the proceedings. She had arrived home only yesterday and had not expected to be faced with a chris-tening ceremony. But Lady Norton had been adamant. Even though Aurelia had shown the good sense not to wed her tiresome brother, Clarice insisted that Aurelia still stand as little Stephen's godmama.

At least, Aurelia thought, it was a diversion from being at the Manor. She had no notion her own house was going to depress her so, with the thought of the empty years stretching out there, a lonely future without—She stiffened, sternly refusing to allow herself to whisper *his* name, even in her heart.

As the vicar moved closer to the baptismal font carved with figures of smiling cherubs, Aurelia eyed the red face of her godchild with considerable sympathy. His tiny fists flailed in a futile attempt to turn his head aside from the frills framing his bonnet.

Aurelia felt equally uncomfortable, although her misery did not stem from her garb, but more from the icy regard of Justin's mama as she inched her way forward for a better view of her grandson. No matter how the rest of the family might feel, Lady Spencer obviously was not accepting the broken engagement with becoming grace.

Aurelia longed for the christening to be over so that she might escape her ladyship's reproachful frowns. The vicar's voice droned on, all but drowned out by young Stephen's howls of disaproval. They had reached the part for Aurelia to utter her own solemn pledges of care for the child when the the door at the far end of the church was flung violently open.

"Stop!" A familiar male voice shouted. "I forbid you to proceed any further."

The startled vicar nigh dropped the child into the font. Aurelia turned with the others to stare in the direction of the chancel. Sunlight filtered through the stained glass windows, so that the figures of Saints Brigid, Catherine, James and Lawrence appeared to regard with mild astonishment the wild-eyed man rushing toward the south transept.

Everard! Aurelia blinked to make certain she was not imagining things. Nay, it was Everard, although in such fashion as she'd never seen him before. His cravat was all but hanging from his neck, and his plain-cut jacket torn and travel-stained. But the ravages to his clothing were as nothing compared to his face. Ramsey's cool, well-bred features were streaked with sweat, his brow knit into the thunderous expression of a man about to commit murder.

Among the astonished assemblage, the vicar was the first to find his voice. "Sir, what is the meaning of this interuption?"

" 'Tis a friend of my brother's." Lady Norton bounded forward a few steps to intercept Everard. Scarce looking at her, Ramsey thrust the young woman out of his path.

Nothing daunted, Clarice demanded, "Everard, why did you not tell me you were coming to attend the christening?"

Lady Spencer muttered something about "scarcely suitably attired."

"Christening?" The word escaped Everard in a strangled choke. Before Aurelia could react, he strode forward and seized her by the shoulders. His blazing fatigue-rimmed blue eyes roved wildly about the baptistry.

"Where is Snape?" he demanded.

Still somewhat dazed by his sudden appearance, Aurelia realized she was gaping. Closing her jaw somewhat, she stammered, "I—I haven't the slightest notion."

"You haven't the—" Everard stopped, his lips tightening into a thin white line. Then he let loose such as astonishing string of curses that Clarice shrieked, covering her ears.

"Are you drunk, Mr. Ramsey, or mad?" Lady Spencer spluttered.

"This is a house of God, sir," the vicar said, looking as wrathful as he could with the squirming infant in his arms.

"The devil!" Everard hissed. Seizing Aurelia by the wrist, he began dragging her down the aisle. Her first impulse was to resist, but after one sidelong glance at Everard's savage expression, she decided it might be best to humor him. She heard Clarice wail before he hauled her through the church doors, "But who is to be godmother for my baby?"

Outside, Everard flung her unceremoniously onto the seat of an ancient farm cart. He leaped up beside her, slapping the reins down against the backs of a pair of dapple-gray horses. Aurelia clutched the side of her seat, but the plodding mares did not look as though they would have charged forward even to please Satan himself. Despite all of Everard's efforts, they trotted through the sleepy village of Aldgate at a very sedate pace.

Aurelia waited until the last straw-thatched cottage was left behind before she dared risk a glance at Everard.

He looked more in control, but a muscle still twitched along his jaw. His dark hair clung to his brow in such achingly familiar disarray, it was all she could do not to brush the silky midnight strands away from his eyes. She had no idea why he had come, but only that her madly pounding heart was excessively glad that he had.

He finally reined the farm horses to a halt, but stared across the flat panorama of hedgerows and stubbly corn fields, not speaking to her. When the silence stretching out between them grew unbearable, Aurelia summoned up the courage to say meekly. "I—I know young Stephen is not the most prepossessing child, but to interrupt his christening—"

"I knew nothing about the babe"—Everard glared at her—"I thought you were about to be married to Augustus Snape."

"You—you thought . . ." Aurelia gasped. "Have you gone completely out of your mind, Everard Ramsey?"

"I do believe that I have. How could I ever have been so taken in! Damn that Justin! I'll roast him alive." Everard stopped muttering curses under his breath long enough to explain. "He told me you had run off with Snape and I, fool that I am, believed him. I've been pursuing you since yesterday, but I smashed up Justin's new phaeton. Serves him right," he added savagely. "Then I could not find another vehicle to hire except this wretched contraption. I have been going half-mad imagining you in Snape's arms."

Aurelia tensed indignantly, her cheeks flushing. "You believed I would marry that—that disgusting toad—permit him to touch me. Indeed, sir, you certainly have a high opinion of my character."

"As high a one as you have of mine, to think I could be guilty of that wager."

Aurelia returned his glare as they both squared off for several seconds. Everard was the first to avert his gaze.

"I believed you were marrying Snape because you had pledged to do so. I couldn't think of any other way you could have prevented him from continuing with the duel."

"Then you are obviously not gifted with as much imagination as Mr. Snape. I painted for him a very grim picture of all those other men you killed."

195

"Those other . . . what other men?"

"Those three men in Norfolk you shot through the head in duels," Aurelia said tartly. "I daresay there have been so many, it has slipped your memory."

"I—I daresay." Some of the rigidity about Everard's mouth relaxed. His eyes softened, studying her in such a way as caused Aurelia's pulses to flutter. She began to have great difficulty remembering she was angry with him.

Another long moment passed before he asked, "Aurelia, can you truly believe that everything that passed between us was the result of a wager?" He tried to make the question sound offhand, but she could sense how much her doubts had pained him, were hurting him still.

"No." She swallowed. It was impossible for her to be less than honest. "Yes, at first I did. You see, 'twas so much easier to believe that than—than . . ."

"Than what?" he prompted.

"Than to believe you could—could have any other reason for wasting your time upon me." Staring down at the wagon's floorboards, she gave a shaky laugh. "You remember me from the old days last winter. Better than anyone else, you should know what I am."

"Yes, I better than anyone." A strange huskiness filled his voice. He seized her in his arms, crushing her hard against his chest. "You are a . . . beautiful . . . exasperating . . . enchanting . . . infuriating little fool." He punctuated each word with a trail of kisses along her hair, her brow, her cheek, until his mouth finally captured hers.

Although she longed for nothing more than to surrender herself to the fierce, sweet pressure of his lips, Aurelia forced herself to draw back, determined to finish her explanation.

"Oh, Everard," she whispered. "I never meant to hurt you that day. It wasn't that I have such a bad opinion of you, but—but of myself. I can't believe that you could—"

"Love you? Desire you? Then I shall prove it to you, if it takes the rest of my life."

His lips covered hers again, slowly at first, as though he would savor every moment, then becoming more demanding. Aurelia thought she should protest his scheme to throw his life away in this fashion, but with the world spinning so dizzily about her, she could only cling to Everard. When he followed up one kiss with another, she began to abandon all notion of persuading him to give up this folly. And by the next kiss, she was firmly convinced herself of the nobleness of Everard's plan.

Long moments later, when she nestled comfortably against his shoulder, she heard him mutter, "Damme, I am nearly as forgetful as Justin."

She felt his arm shift beneath her as he struggled to retrieve something from his coat pocket.

"Here it is." Triumphantly he pulled forth a small ring. Fashioned in the shape of a rose, its petals were delicately wrought of gold polished to a pink hue. "I searched all of London to find it." He smiled tenderly. "You see I did not forget your penchant for roses."

" 'Tis—'tis beautiful," she said. When she raised her hand, he gently slid the ring onto her trembling finger.

"I—I mean, you do wish to marry me, don't you, Aurelia?" Everard groaned. "Lord, what a mull I am making of this. I mean that I am in love with you—"

She laid her fingers against his lips, her eyes brimming with tears and laughter. " 'Tis all right. I do not know when I have had a more charming proposal. Not since—"

"You little witch." With a throaty growl, Everard jerked her back into his embrace. But the sudden movement tumbled over his valise at the bottom of the cart. The contents spilled out, falling across Aurelia's feet. She broke off their kiss long enough to stare in puzzlement at the objects strewing the floor. Before Everard could prevent her, she bent down to right the valise.

197

Amusement quivered at the corners of her mouth. The case contained nothing but as assortment of cravats, and a well-worn deck of cards. She raised the latter, fixing Everard with a look of teasing accusation.

One dark eyebrow jutted upward. "Well, madam, I did pack in some haste."

He took the deck from her, then with a laugh, threw it into the air. The cards fluttered down the lane unnoticed, as Everard pulled her back against him for another long, lingering kiss.

True romance is <u>not</u> hard to find... you need only look as far as FAWCETT BOOKS

27 million Americans can't read a bedtime story to a child.

It's because 27 million adults in this country simply can't read.

Functional illiteracy has reached one out of five Americans. It robs them of even the simplest of human pleasures, like reading a fairy tale to a child.

You can change all this by joining the fight against illiteracy.

Call the Coalition for Literacy at toll-free **1-800-228-8813** and volunteer.

**Volunteer
Against Illiteracy.
The only degree you need
is a degree of caring.**

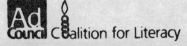

Ad Council Coalition for Literacy

LV-3